# Two Souls United

Etherya's Earth, Book 5.5

By

## REBECCA HEFNER

Cover Design: Anthony O'Brien, BookCoverDesign.store
Editor and Proofreader: Bryony Leah, www.bryonyleah.com

# Contents

*For Sam and Glarys, two supportive characters who deserve their happy ending...*

# A Note from the Author

Hello, lovely readers. I'm thrilled to bring you Sam and Glarys's love story and add to the Etherya's Earth world. I originally wrote this novella for an anthology that never came to fruition, which worked out rather well since this story is perfect for a release date near Valentine's Day.

If you're new to the Etherya's Earth series, please note that this novella falls between Books 5 and 6 in the series and, therefore, *there are a ton of spoilers*. If you'd like to read Book 1 first to get an idea of Etherya's world, make sure you check out **The End of Hatred**. If you're fine with spoilers, then read on, my friends.

I really enjoy writing books with more mature characters and was so excited to see Sam and Glarys get their happy ending after centuries without a soulmate. Here's wishing you happiness too, and I hope you enjoy their sweet, steamy story!

## Chapter 1

S am, son of Raythor, sat in the uncomfortable chair waiting for Lila to walk down the aisle. The sun was high in the clear blue sky, and he closed his eyes, inhaling the fragrant air. Vampyres had only regained the ability to walk in the sun weeks ago. For a thousand years, they'd been cursed by the goddess Etherya to live in darkness, a punishment for their role in the War of the Species with the Slayers. Now that the war had ended and Vampyre King Sathan and Slayer Queen Miranda were married, the goddess had finally rescinded the curse. So thankful to feel the warmth on his skin, Sam basked in the glorious rays.

"Isn't it magnificent?" a melodic voice asked beside him.

Lifting his lids, he smiled at Glarys. The house manager for the sprawling Vampyre royal estate at Astaria was a lovely woman, and he was happy he'd found a seat next to her at the wedding. He'd met her a few times when he'd come to eat dinner at the estate, and the food she prepared was heavenly. Although Vampyres relied on Slayer blood for sustenance, Sam had always enjoyed food and had never tasted anything like Glarys's succulent dishes.

"Amazing," he said, smiling. "I'd almost given up hope."

"For some reason, I never did. Somehow, I knew our people would find a way to end the war. After that, I was sure Etherya would let us walk in the sun again."

"I admire your optimism."

Light blue eyes sparkled as she grinned up at him. "I've always been pretty optimistic. It seems like a waste to be otherwise, right?"

Giving a nod, he said, "It sure does. Life should be lived to the fullest and all that jazz."

"Exactly." The tips of her fangs rested upon her bottom lip as she beamed up at him, and Sam felt a tiny jolt as his heartbeat quickened. Realization swept over him as he envisioned her scraping the tiny points over the vein at his neck... and then piercing the skin as she drank from him.

Processing his attraction to the kindhearted adopted family member of the Vampyre royals, Sam let the sentiment settle in. He certainly didn't expect to feel desire for her, but his body's reaction was undeniable.

Lila chose that moment to walk down the aisle, saving Sam from further analysis. As the ceremony progressed, the stub of his arm tingled as if it wanted to reach for her.

Sam had lost his arm in the Awakening but still felt the limb's presence on occasion. Nolan, the physician at Astaria, called it "phantom arm" and informed Sam he would most likely feel the sensation indefinitely. It was a stark reminder that he'd never quite be whole.

Glancing down at Glarys, he wondered if the sight of the missing limb bothered her. She simply grinned up at him, giving him a wink as Latimus and Lila exchanged their vows, and his throat tightened. She was so pretty, her cheekbones slightly reddened from the sun, and Sam reveled in the moment.

For the first time in so very long, Sam was attracted to a woman. Embracing the feeling, he settled into the chair to watch the ceremony.

Glarys flitted around the ballroom of the huge castle at Astaria making sure glasses were full and empty plates were removed. Doting on people was one of her favorite pastimes, and she was masterful at it. Perhaps that was why she excelled at running the large royal estate. Sathan's father, King Markdor, had hired her centuries ago, before her husband died, and she'd become part of the family. Since she and Victor never had children, her window had closed, leaving her with a soft spot in her heart for the royal Vampyre siblings, whom she loved as her own.

Glarys had gone through her immortal change at sixty-five years old, locking her into a body that was less agile and more withered than most. There was no rhyme or reason as to when a person went through their immortal change, but many Vampyres experienced it in their twenties or thirties.

Sighing, Glarys caught a glimpse of her reflection in the kitchen window as she washed the dishes, inwardly remarking that she looked like an old lady. Her short hair was white as snow, and stubborn little laugh lines extended from her eyes. At least her irises were blue, and the wrinkles weren't that noticeable. She had long, black lashes surrounding her ice-blue eyes and hoped that made her somewhat passable. Telling herself to release the ridiculous musings and get back to work, she finished washing the dishes and set everything in the rack to dry.

Turning, her gaze fell upon Sam, and she gasped. He held up his hand, palm out, looking contrite.

"Sorry, Glarys, I didn't mean to scare you. Jack sent me back here to see if there's any orange juice. He said you squeeze it fresh, and I think he might be addicted to it."

Wiping her hands on the towel before throwing it on the counter, she trailed to the refrigerator and pulled out the pitcher. "I made some just for him. Somehow, I knew he'd ask for it. Want to grab a cup out of the cabinet?"

"Sure." He turned, opening the cabinet and searching inside.

Glarys took the opportunity to steal a glance at his broad back and delicious butt in his dress pants. His tapered waist was accentuated by the black belt he wore, and she breathed a tiny sigh, wishing she could unbuckle it and discover what was inside. Of course, the probability of that happening was slim to none, so she waited, smiling when he approached her with the glass.

She poured a generous portion for his nephew, Jack. Lila and Latimus's adopted son was hands-down the cutest kid on the planet with his freckled face and mop of red hair. Studying Sam, she realized his features mimicked his nephew's. Reddish-blond hair sat above firm features and lightly freckled skin. Deep brown eyes seemed to pool like melted chocolate as he grinned.

"That's real nice of you to make this for Jack. I know he appreciates it."

"Of course," she said, waving her hand and turning to put the drink back in the fridge. "He's stolen my heart, the little munchkin. I'd do just about anything to see that crooked smile of his."

Turning back, she saw Sam's gaze lift and wondered if he'd been staring at her backside. Glarys always carried an additional ten pounds she never had the energy to shed despite wanting to. Maintaining an estate as large as Astaria was exhausting, and she usually fell into bed each night already half-asleep.

"You look pretty in your dress," he said, eyes roaming over her blue frock as she damn near shivered. Telling herself he was just being kind, she gave a slight curtsy.

"Thank you, sir," she teased. "You look wonderful too. I wouldn't be surprised if one of the aristocratic ladies snatched you up for a dance."

His features scrunched. "I've never really had much use for aristocrats. Find them kind of haughty. Except for Lila. She's a damn saint. And Latimus is pretty great too."

"Lila has always been such a sweet girl. I'm so happy she and Latimus finally decided to act on their feelings. It's so beautiful. Isn't true love amazing?"

"It is." His eyebrows drew together. "Lila told me you were married before."

"Yes," she said, trailing her fingers over the counter. "Victor was a lovely man. He was a winemaker and supplied the king with several barrels at the Awakening. Sadly, he was slain, as so many others were."

"That's how I lost my arm," Sam said, lifting the stub. "I was a young soldier and tried like hell to fight back. It got sliced clean off with a poison-tipped blade that rendered my self-healing abilities useless."

"I'm so sorry," she said, taking a step toward him. "Does it still hurt?"

"Nah," he said, shaking his head. "It hasn't hurt in a long time. Still tingles sometimes just to remind me it was once there, I guess."

Chuckling, she bit her lip. "Well, nothing like a good reminder."

Kind eyes studied her. "Do you miss your husband?"

A small sigh escaped her lips. "Every damn day. I miss being in love. Having someone to love me back. Sadly, I don't think I'll ever experience that again. He was a wonderful man."

"I'm real sorry, Glarys."

She smiled, realizing she found his colloquial way of talking quite endearing. Many who frequented the castle were quite formal, and Sam's easygoing natural charm was refreshing.

"Thank you."

Gesturing with the glass, he said, "Well, I'll stop bothering you so you can get back to work. Lila said to tell you to stop working but also said it wouldn't do any good. I think she wants you to have some fun."

"Working is fun for me," Glarys said with a shrug. "It gives me purpose."

"I hear that." He took a step toward the door and then pivoted back. "I really enjoy talking to you, Glarys. Maybe we can find a time to talk again. I mean, if you want to."

She almost swallowed her tongue, overcome with excited surprise. Was it possible that Sam was attracted to her? If so, what the heck should she do? She hadn't been romantically involved with anyone since Victor, and the thought was terrifying for some reason. Choking on the fear, she said, "Of course. Bring Jack over anytime. I know he loves pasta. The three of us could eat together and chat."

His brown eyes roved over her. "Me and Jack. Yeah. Okay, sounds good." Disappointment laced his tone, and she wanted to kick herself. "See you later." Lifting the glass in a salute, he exited the kitchen.

Falling against the counter, Glarys lifted her eyes to the ceiling and rubbed her forehead. "Way to go, Glarys. Now he thinks you're not interested. Good grief." Realizing she'd ruined her first foray into romance in centuries, she blew a breath between puffed cheeks. Chalking it up to a lesson learned, she resumed working, hoping it would clear her head of the images of Sam's broad shoulders and sexy smile.

## Chapter 2

Glarys continued to see Sam over the years, mostly when he joined the royal family for dinners. For immortals, time was a slow-moving constant, and the years bled together with stable regularity. After their conversation in the kitchen at Lila's bonding ceremony, Glarys held out hope Sam might ask to spend some time with her again.

Vowing she wouldn't blow it if he did, she eventually realized he wasn't going to make the move. Unsure whether she'd inadvertently portrayed disinterest or perhaps misconstrued his sentiments, she carried on, immersed in her busy life. After all, she adored the royal siblings and their children, and taking care of them brought her immense joy.

But eventually, they all began to create families of their own. Sathan started to divide his time between Astaria and Uteria, leaving the house devoid of his kingly duties. Latimus moved to Lynia, and Arderin married and moved to the human world. And then, her sweet Heden fell for a human. Overcome with joy that he'd found his soulmate, his announcement he was moving to the human world all but broke Glarys's heart. On the day before his relocation, he found her in the kitchen.

"How am I going to live without you, Glarys?" he asked, eyes sparkling as he smiled down at her. "You're the love of my life."

"Oh, stop it," she said, swatting him with the dish towel. "You and your brothers always tease me. Sofia is a wonderful cook and she'll treat you just fine. I'm so glad you found her, sweet boy."

Heden took her hand, squeezing as he spoke reverent words. "You're so special, Glarys. I never knew my mother, but I thank Etherya every day that you were here to raise us. You deserve to be cherished, and I want so badly for you to be happy."

"I'm happy, son," she said, palming his cheek. "Don't you worry about me."

"I do worry," he said, pulling her into an embrace. "I love you, Glarys."

"I love you too," she whispered, the words true to the core of her soul. "Go make some babies for me to dote on, okay?"

Chuckling, he pulled back. "I'm going to try like hell. I mean, trying's the best part."

She playfully whacked him with the towel again, understanding how much she would miss his gentle jibing. When he drove off in the four-wheeler the next day, he all but took a piece of her heart with him.

Glarys still enjoyed overseeing the large compound, although it was now bereft of the vibrant life it once held. Each day, the duties brought her less joy until she realized she was lonely. It was a strange feeling—and one she hadn't experienced in many centuries. Determined to push through, she began searching for ways to be more involved with the family now that they were scattered across the kingdom. Jack loved pasta, so Glarys began to make a huge vat for him once a month, which she brought to Lynia. It gave her an excuse to have dinner with Jack, Lila, and Latimus as well as Sam, who would come every so often.

Glarys had almost convinced herself she'd eradicated her tiny wisps of desire for the man, but deep inside, she knew that to be a lie. Each time he showed for dinner, her heartbeat would accelerate, and she would feel a burst of pure joy inside her chest. Silly, but it existed all the same. Reminding herself a harmless crush was nothing to be embarrassed about, she carried on, hoping the man didn't notice the flush of her cheeks when he trained that gorgeous brown gaze on her. No—he seemed completely unfazed by her, confirming she'd all but imagined any hint of mutual attraction all those years ago at the bonding ceremony.

One night, a few months after Heden moved to the human world, Glarys joined them for dinner at Latimus and Lila's house at Lynia. The meal was filled with wine and wonderful conversation as well as their three adorable children: Jack, Adelyn, and Symon. Moments like this spurred such gratefulness in Glarys's heart, reminding her how lucky she was to be a part of their family. During these dinners, the loneliness seemed so far away, and she reveled in their comradery.

"We're so happy you're staying with us now that Milakos has decided to move to Takelia and join the council," Latimus said. "You're welcome to stay as long as you need, Sam."

"Thank you," Sam said as he spooned out some pasta sauce. "Council members get their own security detail funded by the compound, as you know, so he no longer needs me as private security. I'm going to take a few weeks off since the job was pretty intense, and then I'll find something new. I'll be out of your hair in no time," he said, winking at Lila.

Lila wrinkled her nose. "I wish you'd just move in with us, but I know you crave your independence, so I won't badger you."

"If you need help finding another post, let me know," Latimus said. "I know a plethora of stuffy aristocrats who don't know the first thing about protecting themselves and would hire you in a second."

"Daddy hates aristocrats," Adelyn said, staring up at Sam. "He says they're titled."

"That's *entitled*, sweetie, and most of them are," Latimus said, shrugging.

"Daddy doesn't hate anyone, does he?" Lila corrected, shooting a look at her husband. "We don't believe in hate in this house."

"That's right," Latimus said, although his tone was less than thrilled. "I agree with Momma so she'll keep kissing me. I've learned that's the best way to make that happen."

Lila scrunched her features. "Very funny. But let's remember to be kind, okay, guys?"

They all murmured their agreement while Glarys enjoyed the interplay.

"Well, thanks, Latimus," Sam said, his full lips curving into a smile. "I'll let you know when I'm ready."

The dinner progressed until the hour grew late, and Glarys prepared to head home. As she reached for her light jacket hanging by the door, a strong arm entered her line of view and grabbed the coat instead. Turning, she smiled up at Sam.

"Thought I could help you with your jacket," he said, his expression kind. "But it's probably not that helpful since I only have one arm."

"It's lovely," she said, threading her arm through the jacket as he shimmied it over her skin. Rotating, she slid the other arm in and tugged it tight across her abdomen. "Perfect. What a gentleman you are."

"Happy to oblige," he said, giving her a mock salute. "It was real nice to see you tonight, Glarys. Hope you make it home safely."

Before she could speak, Latimus appeared. "Ready for me to drive you to the train?"

"Yes," she said, shooting Sam one last smile. "Have a good night."

He gave a nod, and she pivoted to walk down the front porch steps with Latimus. As he drove the four-wheeler to the Lynia train station, Glarys couldn't shake the image of Sam's handsome face and muscled arm.

"How are you doing at Astaria, Glarys?" Latimus asked. "You know you can come live with us anytime."

"Thank you, dear," she said, exiting the vehicle. Although the offer had been issued repeatedly, she didn't want to be a burden on the young family. "Someone has to take care of that big ol' house, especially since you've all left me."

He pulled her into an embrace, kissing her white hair. "I worry about you, Glarys."

"I'm fine, boy," she said, drawing back and waving a dismissive hand. "But you're very sweet. Now, let me get on home. I don't want to miss the train. Talk to you in a few days." Keeping her voice light, she waggled her fingers as she trailed down the stairs.

As the train chugged along, she sat in the almost empty car figuring most people were home with their families since it was late. At least it was quiet and she could possibly catch a catnap before they pulled into Astaria's station. Closing her eyes, she rested her head on the seat.

Suddenly, the train ground to a halt, and her lids snapped open. Yells and cries of war sounded from outside the train car, and terror seized Glarys's veins. Standing, she pulled the handgun from her bag. Latimus had given it to her decades ago and trained her on how to use it, but she was no expert. Still, she would wield the weapon valiantly against any enemy who tried to harm her. She might not have the most exciting life, but it was a life she damn well wanted to keep living.

The Deamons stormed the train, Glarys realizing they must've been sent by Bakari. The outcast royal sibling had built a Deamon army, spawned from the prisoners he'd freed at Takelia, and they were now a new foe for the Vampyres and Slayers.

Two male passengers began to fight the beady-eyed creatures, and Glarys lifted the gun, firing at one and catching him in the abdomen. Pride surged through her as he fell to the ground. More fighting ensued, and she thought she saw the immortal troops out of the corner of her eye. Thankful that Latimus's soldiers were well-trained and had responded so quickly, she whirled around when something grabbed her neck. As she stared into one of the Deamon's eyes, he whacked his forehead against hers.

The last thing she saw before she succumbed to unconsciousness was the malicious curl of his lips, cruel and menacing.

## Chapter 3

Sam tapped his foot against the floor, hand covering his mouth as he anxiously waited in Latimus and Lila's living room. He'd been about to turn in when Latimus's cell rang. The massive soldier had informed them that the trains were being attacked by Bakari's Deamon forces.

Fear for Glarys had immediately surged in Sam's heart. He'd offered to go with Latimus to help the troops, but the commander had asked him to stay and keep an eye on Lila and the kids. Now, the kids were upstairs sleeping, and he and Lila waited, worried and pensive.

The front door swung open, and Latimus walked in, gently leading Glarys, who looked unstable on her feet. Sam and Lila rushed over, and she shooed them away.

"Please don't make a fuss," she said as Sam noticed the shiner beginning to form under her eye and the huge knot on her forehead. "I wasn't hurt at all. Latimus really should've let me go home."

"No way, Glarys," Latimus said, taking her jacket and hanging it up as she massaged her head. "You were hit pretty hard, and I'm not sending you home alone. Sathan's at Uteria, and the castle only has the barebone staff. You're staying here, and I'm putting my foot down."

"Oh, fine. I don't have the energy to argue anyway. I'm just shaken. That was a lot of energy for this old lady."

"She can have my guest room," Sam said, stepping forward and offering out his arm. "Please, Glarys, I insist. I'll lead you there."

"Okay."

Gritting his teeth at the purple bruise forming on her head, he vowed to strangle every Deamon who had touched her. Gently taking her hand, he led her into the room and turned down the bed while she removed her shoes. Lila entered behind them, and they both ushered her into bed.

"Nolan says we need to check on you every few hours, so we might wake you up," Lila said, tenderly wiping the white hair from Glarys's temple. "I promise we'll take care of you."

"I don't need anything, dear," she said, shaking her head on the pillow. "Please don't go out of your way." Her lids blinked slowly a few times before fluttering closed. "I'll be fine tomorrow," she murmured as she drifted off.

Lila lifted her fist to her mouth, and Sam saw the tears forming. "Come on, sweetie," he said, taking her hand. "She's out of danger now. We need to let her rest."

Lila clasped his hand, and he led her back to the living room, where Latimus was speaking to Slayer Commander Kenden. Shutting off his phone, he ran a hand over his slick black hair.

"Those bastards attacked three train lines tonight. Bakari is growing bolder. Ken and I will begin implementing updated posts and training tomorrow."

"Thank the goddess Glarys is okay," Lila said, hand over her heart as she sat beside Sam. "Lattie, we have to assign a bodyguard to her. I know Bakari can't infiltrate the goddess's protective wall at Astaria, but I'm terrified for her safety."

"I asked her again tonight to live with us, but she won't budge. She's pretty stubborn and independent, which is one of the things we all love most about her. I mean, we can't force her to move here."

"I can do it." The words left Sam's mouth before he even realized he'd uttered them.

"What's that, Sam?" Lila asked.

"Assign me as Glarys's bodyguard. I'm free now that my private security post for Milakos has ended. I'll guard Glarys."

Latimus and Lila exchanged a look. Arching his brows as he considered, Latimus said, "It's not a bad idea. I could pay you out of the military funds since she's technically a member of the royal family. I don't think I'd get any pushback at all from Sathan or Miranda."

"I don't care about money," Sam said, waving his hand. "I'd just really like to keep her safe. If she's determined to keep living at Astaria, I'll guard her."

"I think it's a lovely idea," Lila said, grasping his hand. "And of course Latimus will arrange for you to be paid. I would feel so much better knowing you're around to keep her safe, Sam."

"Me too," Latimus said with a nod. "Do you mind relocating to Astaria for a while? I don't know how long the post will be, but it could be years before we defeat Bakari. Are you up for that?"

"Yes. I was planning on moving to wherever my new post eventually took me. I can move to Astaria just as easily."

"Since you'll be guarding Glarys, you'll have to live at the castle. There are a lot of unoccupied rooms there, mine and Heden's being the most recently vacated. You can have your pick."

Sam's breathing quickened as he comprehended what he'd just signed up for. But he'd been in private security for years now and was extremely capable. With his missing arm, he could no longer fight in the military, but his skill set came in quite handy as a bodyguard. And he'd get to spend a plethora of time with Glarys. Although she'd made it quite clear she wasn't interested in him romantically, she was still an amazing woman whom he liked very much. His clumsy attempts to spend one-on-one time with her had been met with suggestions of involving others, which he understood was a nice way of brushing him off.

He couldn't say he blamed her. Although she was a paid servant of the royal family, she was a white-collar worker, one who'd been educated along with the aristocrats she served. Sam could barely read and write since he'd always been more interested in becoming a soldier than studying. His lack of formal education, compounded by the fact he was missing an arm, probably wasn't all that attractive to Glarys, who was surrounded by royalty at every turn. Still, he had an affinity toward her and would strive to protect her.

"It would be an honor to keep her safe. Do you think she'll be resistant to having a bodyguard?"

Latimus exchanged a look with Lila. "Maybe. She's a tough one. But Lila and I will insist upon it, don't you worry about that."

"Good. I'll sleep on the couch tonight. Y'all go ahead and go on to bed. We can tell her tomorrow."

Standing, Lila took his face between her hands. "You're too good, Sam." She softly kissed his lips. "Thank you."

"Of course."

Lila and Latimus trailed up the stairs, leaving Sam in the darkened living room to process what he'd committed to.

L ila watched her bonded mate remove his shirt as she brushed her hair. Every so often, her eyes would drift to his magnificent chest, reflected in the mirror, and her body hummed with desire. By the goddess, he was glorious. Biting her lip, she wondered if he was in the mood for sexy times since he was most likely exhausted from his efforts with the troops earlier.

He removed his pants and underwear, standing tall and naked as he slowly approached her. Finding her gaze in the mirror, his ice-blue eyes locked onto hers.

"Are you staring at me, little temptress?"

"Yes," she whispered, baring her neck so he could place butterfly kisses over the pulsing vein.

"Good wives would let their tired husbands sleep after such a long day."

Setting down the brush, she arched a brow. "You know I'm only good in public. In here, anything goes."

"Which is why this bedroom is my favorite place in the whole damn world," he said, waggling his eyebrows as she chuckled. "Sam's offer was interesting," he murmured against her skin.

Nodding, she tried to concentrate on the conversation—difficult, since her mate was doing something amazing with his tongue against her skin. "I can't believe I didn't see it. He's smitten with her."

"I've noticed for several years now," Latimus said, sliding his arm around her waist and drawing her still-clothed body into his.

"You have? Why didn't you tell me? I would've tried to matchmake for sure."

"Once you've secretly longed for someone yourself, it becomes easy to see it in another man."

Emotion filled her lavender irises as she clutched his hand above her abdomen. "I wish I had known. So much time wasted where we could've loved each other."

His fangs nipped her earlobe, causing her to shiver. "We won't let them make our mistakes. Hopefully, their newfound proximity will lead to something more. And it will keep her safe, which is paramount."

Sighing, she tilted her face to his. "When did you become so romantic?"

"When you turned me into a lovesick sap." Pressing his erection into her lower back, his fingers found the button of her jeans, releasing it before sliding the zipper down. Gliding his fingers over her mound, he found her slick warmth. "Now, be a good girl and bend over the dresser, honey."

Her fangs squished her lip as she grinned. "Someone's bossy."

"Do you want me, sweetheart? Because I'm desperate for you. Let me take you while you give me that sexy smile in the mirror. Come on, honey."

Reaching behind her back, she gripped his straining shaft. "Oh, my, you do feel ready."

"You little temptress. Bend over."

Shimmying out of her jeans and thong, she pulled her shirt over her head and tossed it to the floor. The last coherent memory she had was spreading her palms wide over the dresser before her bonded's skillful loving erased every other musing in her aroused mind.

# Chapter 4

Glarys's lids fluttered open, and she immediately reached for her pounding forehead. "Ouch."

"You've got a really bad bump, Glarys," Lila said, sitting on the bed, concern lacing her tone. "It's probably going to hurt for a few days even with your self-healing body."

"Well, I guess it could've been worse, so I can live with a headache." Struggling to sit up, she realized she was still wearing yesterday's dress. "Oh, my. I've got to get home and shower. Miranda's having some of Tordor's friends over for a sleepover tonight, and I've got to prepare the mansion."

"Miranda's staying at Uteria tonight, and Jana is going to host there," Lila said, referencing Glarys's counterpart at the Slayer castle. "You just need to focus on resting and healing."

Feeling off-balance, she struggled to stand as her legs threatened to turn to jelly. "Whoa, there," Sam said, rushing to her side. "Lean on me."

"Thank you," she said, wondering why he was in her room. For the love of the goddess, she must look hideous. "I'm fine. Just a little woozy."

"Sam will get you home and make sure you're all set, Glarys. He's volunteered to be your bodyguard for however long this conflict with Bakari lasts."

Glarys's heart slammed in her chest. "Oh, that's not necessary."

"It's already done," he said, giving her a sheepish grin. "Latimus processed the paperwork and everything. I'm trained in private security and promise you'll be safe."

Feeling her knees buckle, she sat back on the bed. Of course the man she had a terrible crush on would sign up to guard her when she was in her weakest state and probably looked like a damn invalid. Annoyed, she tried again to dissent.

"I'm a grown woman and am perfectly capable of taking care of myself."

"It's non-negotiable, Glarys," Latimus said, arms crossed over his thick chest as he stood in the doorway. "You've never shied away from giving me much-needed stern lectures, so don't think I won't reciprocate. Sam is now your assigned bodyguard, and he's vowed to protect you. I care more about your safety than you being mad at me. Sorry." He shrugged and grinned.

"All this fuss for little ol' me... I just think it's silly."

"I'm honored to ensure your safety, Glarys," Sam said in his silken baritone, causing parts deep in her body that she hadn't felt for ages to flare to life. "This doesn't have to be a big thing. I'm pretty low-key and promise I won't restrict you."

Inhaling deeply, she contemplated the three people who stared at her with such concern. "Oh, fine. If you want to waste your time watching a boring old lady cook and clean, that's your life. I'm ready to get home, so, if we're going, let's go."

Sam beamed at her, offering his arm so she could balance. They ambled out the door, Sam hopping behind the wheel of a four-wheeler after she was situated in the passenger seat.

"Tell the kids I'll come see them when I'm healed. I don't want them to see all these bruises on my face."

"Will do." Lila gave her a firm embrace before they began the trek toward Astaria.

"You don't have to do this, Sam," Glarys said, noticing his gorgeous profile as he drove. "I'm sure there's some other security job you would enjoy more."

"Good try, but you're stuck with me," he said, flashing her a grin. "We're going to get you better, and I'm moving to Astaria as your bodyguard. I'll do my best not to drive you nuts."

Settling in, she realized that was the least of her worries. No—Glarys was more consumed with the idea her attraction to him would continue to grow until she did something embarrassing, such as beg him to kiss her. Determined to keep her desire in check, she accepted her fate.

Two days after the attack, Glarys pushed the flesh around her shiner with the pads of her fingers. It was still a bit swollen and looked absolutely terrible —like a dark half-moon under her eye— but that meant it was healing. Two more days, and she hoped her self-healing body would eliminate it.

Since she'd gone through her change late in life, her self-healing properties worked a bit slower than those of a Vampyre locked in a younger body. The abilities were still appreciated, though, since Slayers didn't possess such powers. Like humans, they could be killed instantly, even though they were immortal, and Glarys was thankful her body would eventually return to its regular state.

Craving normalcy, she headed downstairs to begin her daily chores. As she was wiping down the marble island countertop in the expansive kitchen, Sam sauntered in, looking absolutely delicious in jeans and a black T-shirt. His shoulders were broad above his trim waist, and she'd bet anything a six-pack adorned his taut abdomen.

"Good morning," she said, hoping he couldn't see the vein pulsing at her neck. "Would you like some coffee?"

"Sure would," he said, lowering onto one of the stools at the counter. "You've already figured out what makes me tick, Glarys. Good coffee and nice conversation. You're a master at both."

"Why, thank you," she said, pouring him a cup with cream and one sugar since that was what he'd taken yesterday morning. Placing it in front of him, she rested her hands on the countertop. "Well, I need to go to town today. I guess you're going to accompany me?"

"Sure am," he said, eyes sparkling as he sipped the coffee. "Are you still secretly pissed you have to put up with me?"

"Of course not," she said, playfully swatting him with her dish towel. "I just think guarding me must be an incredibly dull use of your time. At least Latimus is paying you. Otherwise, I'd feel terrible."

He took another sip as he studied her. "Actually, I really like spending time with you, Glarys. I was pretty sure you'd figured that out by now."

Heat flooded her cheeks, and she tried to keep herself from covering them to hide her blush. "Oh, well, that's nice of you to say. Most young people I know enjoy hanging out with other people their age."

Setting down his cup, he pondered her. "I don't want to overstep here, but why do you keep calling yourself old?"

"Oh, I..." Feeling like an idiot, her gaze fell to the counter as she absently wiped it with the cloth. "Well, it's obvious I went through my change later in life. I've already had a marriage and lived so many decades before being frozen in my immortality."

He squinted. "When did you go through your change? Sixty?"

She breathed a laugh. "Sixty-five, you charmer. But thank you."

"I went through at forty-three. So I'd lived a few decades myself."

Her eyes roved over his muscled arm and chiseled face. He was extraordinarily handsome and didn't appear a day over forty. "Well, you look young compared to me."

"But we're both over one thousand years old in the scheme of things. So even though you were born a few centuries before me, we've certainly caught up to each other now."

"Yes, but I'll always look like this," she said, pointing at her slightly wrinkled face and white hair. "I could dye it but just never really cared enough to do it."

"I like your hair," he said, eyes narrowing as he studied her. "It looks real soft."

"Oh," she said, patting her curls as she tried not to faint at the reverent compliment. "Well, thank you. It's easy to maintain, so I just leave it."

Finishing the last of the coffee, he gave a nod and stood. "Well, I'll let you finish what you need here, and then we can head to the main square at ten a.m.?"

"Sure thing. That sounds perfect. I'll meet you outside the back door."

He flashed a grin before pivoting to leave. Only a moment later, he called her name from the doorway.

"Yes?" She noticed the whites of his knuckles on the frame as he seemed to hesitate.

"I'm happy you'll always look like you do now. I think you're real pretty." With a tilt of his head, he said, "See you at ten."

When he'd disappeared through the door, Glarys placed her hand over the space where her neck met her chest, wondering what the hell had just happened. Her new bodyguard, whom she was all but lusting over, had complimented her. Was it out of kindness or a mutual attraction? Glarys had no idea since she hadn't been involved with anyone romantically since Victor, but suddenly, she was aching to find out.

# Chapter 5

G larys had a lovely time at the market with Sam, noting how attentive he was. As they strolled through the farmers market, he urged her to lead and ensured he walked between her and the street. As the empty bags she'd brought became heavy, he offered to carry them, stacking them on his arm.

"I can carry the bags, Sam," she said, smiling up at him under the blue sky. "You're my bodyguard, not my servant. I don't want to take advantage of you."

"A gentleman never lets a lady carry her own bags," he said, lifting them as his sinewed muscles strained underneath. Flashes of him working that arm and his long, broad fingers around her nether regions caused her to clear her throat. "Please, let me help you. I remember you telling me that working made you happy. Well, doing my part to help makes me feel the same way."

"Okay," she said, wondering if she'd ever met someone so kind. "I only need a few more items, and we'll head home."

Once back at the castle, she threw herself into baking cupcakes for Symon's upcoming birthday party. After that, she decided she needed to clean the gym since the kids would want to play there if it rained. Donning her yoga pants and an old T-shirt—her most comfortable housecleaning attire—she headed to the gym and gasped when she entered.

Sam was punching the bag with his arm in sure strokes. Shirtless, beads of sweat ran down his magnificent chest and abdomen to the waistband of his black athletic shorts. His feet were bare, showcasing the springy brown hair on his legs. Overcome with desire, all she could do was stare.

"Hey," he said, straightening. "I'm almost finished. Did you come to work out?"

"Oh, no, although I probably should." Glancing down at her stomach, Glarys prayed her love handles weren't too pronounced. "I just came to clean. I can come back."

"It's fine," he said, grabbing the water canister on the bench and taking several gulps. The line of his throat was glossy with sweat, his Adam's apple bobbing as he swallowed. God, but she wanted to bite him there. Just close her eyes, stick her fangs in his neck, and lose herself in his taste.

Realizing she was staring like an idiot, she ran her hand over her hair. "I'll come back. Take all the time you need." Pivoting, she told herself not to run from the room.

His warm hand slid over her shoulder before she could exit. "I don't want to mess up your routine, Glarys. I'm the visitor here. Please, I'd feel terrible if you rearranged your schedule for me. I know you keep a tight ship in this place."

"I do," she said, grinning up at him.

"Okay then. I'm going to shower. See you tomorrow for the trip to Takelia, right?"

She nodded. "We can leave any time after nine a.m. I told Evie I'd be there by ten to prepare the lunch she's having with the council and the donors."

"Perfect." His eyes roved over her face. "Latimus told me Heden left an awesome collection of movies behind in the theater room. I'm going to find one to watch tonight. You're welcome to join me if you're not too tired. Hope to see you there." With one last curve of his full lips, he exited the gym.

Glarys stood frozen for several seconds, allowing her pulse to return to some semblance of normalcy. Sam had now told her she was pretty and asked her to spend time with him. She'd convinced herself he was just being nice—that he wouldn't desire someone who looked more mature—but she'd misread people before. Chewing her lip with her fangs, she contemplated and decided she would indeed watch a movie with him tonight. It would allow her to study him and hopefully figure out if he desired her even half as much as she did him.

S am's heart slammed in his chest when Glarys tentatively rounded the corner into the theater room later that evening. Throwing the blanket aside on the brown leather couch, he rose to meet her.

"Hey," he said, extending his hand and leading her to the couch. "Have a seat here."

She slid into the corner, those apple-ripe cheeks glowing red, and he almost blushed too. Wanting to make her feel comfortable, he sat on the opposite corner and lifted the remote.

"I just started Star Wars. It said Episode IV, but it's actually the first one released. Have you seen it?"

"No," she said, reaching for the blanket located on the shelf of the nearby table. "But Heden was always quoting it. Something about Han Solo and how he was pretty badass. I'm excited to finally see it." Covering herself with the blanket, she settled in.

Pressing play, Sam relaxed back, overcome with her presence and her smell. Her scent reminded him of the pretty purple flowers Latimus had planted for Lila in front of her cottage at Lynia all those years ago. Wispy and full of spring, he reveled in it as they watched the movie.

Always aware of her out of the corner of his eye, he noticed her relax as the movie progressed, shifting her legs onto the couch and eventually stretching them so they almost touched his thigh. Her feet peeked out from the blanket, and blood surged to his shaft at the sight of her red toenails. He'd never really been a toe guy, but hers were absolutely adorable.

During an exciting scene in which Darth Vader was battling Obi-Wan Kenobi, they both jumped at a particularly thrilling exchange, and her feet surged into his leg.

"Oh, sorry!" she said, drawing back her legs. "This is so good!"

Smiling, he surrounded both of her feet with his hand. "It sure is. Heden was right about these movies being fantastic." Scooching toward her, he pulled her feet atop his thigh. Settling back into the couch, he began to massage them as they watched the climax of the movie.

"You don't have to do that," she said, grinning at him as the side of her head rested on the back of the couch. "I didn't mean to kick you."

He dug his thumb into her arch, arousal flaming deep within as her eyes lit with pleasure. "You were on your feet all day and survived a Deamon attack less than a week ago. I think you deserve a good foot massage."

Her breathy sigh surrounded him like a warm blanket. By the goddess, he wanted nothing more than to feel her breath against the shell of his ear...and against his neck as she drank from him...and around his cock before she slid those pink lips over the straining, sensitive skin...

"Well, if you insist, I'm not going to argue."

"I think that's a first from you," he said with a wink. "Relax, honey. I've got you."

When the movie was finished, Sam muted the TV and set the remote aside. Sliding his hand back around her feet, he softly stroked them.

"Your skin is so smooth," he murmured.

Her features scrunched. "If you like my feet, you should feel my neck. I moisturize the hell out of it in hopes of keeping the wrinkles away. I know my body's supposedly locked in time, but I'm not taking any chances."

Gaze locked with hers, his breath began to quicken. Slowly, he placed her feet on the couch and glided toward her. Encircling her arm with his fingers, he tugged her toward him.

"Slide over me," he whispered.

Her blue eyes were wide as the vein in her neck pulsed. "Why?"

"Come on," he said, gently tugging her. "Slide your leg over mine."

White fangs squished the flesh of her lip as she contemplated. Tentatively, she glided her jean-clad leg over his thigh until she straddled him, her hands gripping his shoulders tight, revealing her nervousness.

"You've got me in a death grip there, honey."

"Sorry," she whispered, relaxing her fingers. "I haven't done this in a long time."

Lifting his hand, he placed his palm over the juncture where her neck met her chest. Slowly caressing her, he trailed his hand over her skin, loving how it reddened in its wake.

"You're right," he murmured.

"Hmm?"

"Your skin here is really soft." He continued to stroke her, content to let her relax into the ministrations.

"Sam," she breathed.

"Yes, sweetheart?"

"I think I want you to kiss me."

His lips curved into what must've been the sappiest grin of all time. "Yeah?"

She swallowed thickly before nodding. "I think I remember how to do it."

Chuckling, he cupped her neck, gently urging her closer. "What if I don't know how to do it?"

"You're so handsome," she said, tightening her arms around his neck. "I bet you've kissed all sorts of women."

"Honestly," he said, inching closer to her lips, "I think I've damn near forgotten any woman exists except you, Glarys." Reveling in her quick inhale, he brushed his lips against hers. "In fact, you're all I think about."

"I am?"

Nuzzling her nose, he nodded. "Every damn second of every damn day." Extending his tongue, he swiped it over her lips.

"Oh, god," she moaned, wriggling over his cock and sending jolts of pleasure through his body.

Pressing his lips to hers, he consumed them, unable to hold back any longer.

Glarys settled into a man's body for the first time in so very long. Parts she'd thought to be long dormant flared to life as his magnificent lips moved over hers. The hard jut of his cock against her core through their clothes spurred a rush of moisture between her thighs. Craving contact she'd been so long denied, she shimmied over his straining shaft, reveling in his resulting groan.

"I can smell your arousal," he whispered into her mouth, breaths mingling as he stroked her tongue with his.

"I haven't felt arousal in so long. I wasn't sure if my lady parts still worked."

Chuckling, he kissed her, pulling her bottom lip between his own before changing the angle and plunging his tongue inside. Glarys melted, encircling his neck as she pressed her breasts against his broad chest. Her nipples tingled along with her slick core, which throbbed as she wriggled atop his strong body.

"Man," he whispered, breaking the kiss and resting his forehead upon hers. "You taste so good, honey."

Smiling, she ran her thumb over his lip. "I wasn't sure you wanted me back. I convinced myself you were just being nice."

"Nice?" Arching an eyebrow, he jutted his erection into her mound. "Does that feel nice, sweetheart?"

"Actually, it rather does."

Throwing back his head, he laughed, baring his neck to her. Overcome with desire, she began to trail kisses over his vein.

"I want to drink from you. Goddess, I can't believe I just said that, but it's true."

Threading his fingers through her hair, he gently tugged her head away. "I want that too. So much, Glarys."

Her fangs toyed with her lip. "But you have reservations?"

Sighing, he nodded. "You're really special, and I don't want to cross a line here. First, I need to know if you're okay dating your bodyguard."

"As long as you don't have a problem with it, I don't."

"I feel a calling to protect you," he said, causing something to swell in her chest, "so I'm extremely honored to have this assignment. But I want to speak to Latimus before we take this any further." Her expression must've fallen because he cupped her cheek. "I want to do this right, honey. Bodyguards have fallen for their wards before. I saw it happen all the time at Valeria, and it's not unacceptable in Vampyre culture. But Latimus is paying me to protect you, and I want to make sure he understands my intentions toward you."

She arched a brow, trying to appear sexy. "And what are your intentions?"

Expelling a ragged breath, he slid his thumb over her lip, his gaze focused on her mouth. "To have those sexy fangs plunged into every part of my neck while I'm deep inside your gorgeous body."

Moisture gushed between her legs at the amorous words spoken in his deep baritone. "You want to make love to me?"

"Oh, hell yes. More than I've wanted anything in centuries, honey. I can't believe you haven't realized I'm smitten with you. Why do you think I volunteered so fast to guard you?"

"Because you're altruistic and kind," she said, placing a peck on his lips.

"Eh, maybe." He slid his hand down her body, gliding it over her ass. "Or maybe I had ulterior motives."

"Probably both." Winking, she stroked the thick hair at his temple. "Latimus will

be leading a training at Takelia tomorrow...
you know, if you want to talk to him while
we're there."

"I'll do that."

They stroked each other for a while
before Sam said softly, "Let me carry you
to bed."

"Oh, I can walk," she said, waving a
dismissive hand.

"I know, but this will be more fun." He
waggled his eyebrows. "I wish I had both
arms so I could whisk you upstairs and
hold you tight, but I can still manage with
one. Clench my neck tight."

Following his directive, she gave a little
squeal when he lifted her, carrying her as
if she were weightless while her legs
encircled his waist. "I hope I'm not too
heavy. I swear, I'm going to lose the extra
ten pounds I'm carrying one day."

"You're perfect, honey."

The words shot thrills of pleasure to
every cell in her body.

Once he'd carried her up the stairs, Sam
laid her down, and Glarys's head fell to
the pillow. Sitting by her side, he traced
the healing shiner under her eye.

"It's almost gone."

"Yes. Does it look terrible?"

"No, but I'm really pissed they hurt you."

"I'm fine. I'm a tough old broad."

Melted brown eyes washed over her face. "I can't wait to hold you again," he whispered.

"Tomorrow," she whispered back.

"Tomorrow. But for now..." Lowering, he placed a slow, reverent kiss on her lips. Lifting from the bed, he gave her a salute. "Night, Glarys."

"Night."

Once he'd closed the door behind him, she rolled over and all but screamed into the pillow like a teenager with her first crush. Still overcome with arousal from his ardent kisses, it was hours before she eventually fell asleep.

*Chapter 6*

When the sun rose, Glarys put on one of her most flattering dresses and even applied a little makeup. She rarely wore the stuff but wanted to look pretty for Sam. When he strolled into the kitchen with that lazy swagger, her heart slammed in her chest. He looked delicious in jeans, a brown T-shirt, and boots. A gun was holstered on his waist by his leather belt. Physically restraining from licking her lips in anticipation, she prepared a cup of coffee and set it in front of him.

Mahogany eyes sparkled as he drank it, sitting still while she buzzed around the kitchen. When everything was prepared, she plopped her hands on her hips.

"Well, I had most of the food delivered to Takelia, and all my supplies are packed. You ready?"

"Ready," he said, standing and grabbing the two bags from the counter.

"Should I even try to carry those?"

"Nope." The sexy curve of his lips all but made her gush in her panties. By the goddess, he was handsome. "A gentleman never lets a lady carry her own bags. Let's go."

They sat together on the train to Takelia, her skin warm beneath her dress as it brushed against his side.

"I think green is your color. That dress looks fantastic on you, Glarys."

"Oh, this ol' thing? I just threw it on this morning," she teased, realizing he'd probably already guessed she spent extra time primping.

"Well, you look pretty as always. I like the stuff on your face," he said, circling his hand in front of his face.

"It's called makeup, and thank you very much. I might have put on extra for you."

She thought he uttered a small growl. "You don't need it, but I sure do like the thought of you thinking of me in your bedroom."

"Oh, you flirt," she said, swatting his chest.

He placed a peck on her head, and she settled into his side, loving their interplay. When they arrived at Takelia, Evie and Lila met them at the station.

"You're a godsend, Glarys," Evie said, hugging her. "These donors are so freaking demanding, but I need their money, and half of them refused to come unless I had those damn crab cakes and bacon-wrapped melons you prepared last time. You're a victim of your own success. Thanks for making the trip."

"I'm happy to do it, and it warms my heart that both the Slayer and Vampyre aristocrats enjoy my cooking."

"Hello, Sam," Evie said, arching her scarlet eyebrow. "My, oh, my...there are just all sorts of lascivious thoughts circling about today. Have you been a naughty bodyguard?"

Sam chuckled, remembering Evie was quite powerful and possessed the ability to read others' thoughts. "Now, Evie, you know I'm too much of a stickler for protocol to cross the line too far...even if Glarys looks like a million dollars in her pretty green dress."

"Oh, will you both stop?" Glarys held her palms to her flaming cheeks. "This is all sorts of embarrassing."

"Come on," Lila said, sliding her arm around Glarys's shoulders and leading her toward the castle. "Those two are just having fun, but you do look really stunning today, Glarys. The shiner's all but gone."

"Thank you, sweetie. That's nice of you to say to this old lady."

"I don't think Sam sees you that way." Lila chucked her golden eyebrows.

Walking up the stairs, they entered the mansion and began to trail to the kitchen.

"We'll see. He's going to speak to Latimus while we're here. Wants to ask permission to date me while he's guarding me. It sounds silly when I say it out loud, but I appreciate the sentiment."

"Oh, that's wonderful." Pulling her close, Lila whispered, "I knew it. You two are perfect for each other."

"Are you ladies talking about me?" Sam asked, smiling as he filtered in and placed the bags on the counter.

"Less talking and more working," Glarys said, picking up the cloth on the countertop and using it to shoo them all away. "I need to get to work, and you all need to give me space. Now, go on, so I can fix this spread for Evie."

"You're a saint." Evie placed a kiss on her forehead before breezing from the room. "Call me if you need anything."

"I'll take you to Latimus," Lila said to Sam.

Nodding, he walked over and squeezed Glarys's upper arm. "Let me know if you need any help."

Inwardly sighing at his thoughtfulness, she nodded. "Good luck. I feel like we're teenagers asking permission to go to prom."

His deep chuckle enveloped her. "Feels like it." With a nod, he left the room with Lila.

Opening the fridge to assess the supplies she'd requested, Glarys got down to business.

S am found Latimus atop a small hill, leading the soldiers in drills. Placing his fingers between his lips, the commander gave a loud whistle and yelled, "Take five, soldiers!"

"Didn't mean to interrupt you," Sam said.

"They needed a break anyway. How are things at Astaria? Is Glarys feeling okay?"

"She's fine," Sam said, sliding his hand into his back pocket. "But I want to talk to you about something."

Latimus's eyebrow lifted. "About the fact you've been pining for her for years?"

Huffing a laugh, he nodded. "Yep. That would be it."

"Did you finally make a move? Lila and I were thrilled when you offered to guard her."

"I made a move," he said, looking out across the meadow. "Haven't been with a woman in a long time. It took a while to convince myself I was still whole after losing this." Lifting the stub of his arm, he felt his lips thin. "Still have to convince myself some days, but it's gotten easier over the centuries. Glarys is so sweet and pretty and probably a hell of a lot smarter than me, but she seems to like me anyway."

"That's fantastic, Sam," Latimus said, patting his shoulder with friendly affection. "I know she's been lonely since she lost Victor, and we all worry about her being alone in the mansion. She's like a mother to all of us. I wish you both happiness."

"I don't want to overstep my bounds. If you think this crosses an ethical line, dating her while I'm employed as her private security detail, I'll resign."

"Hell, I can name so many of my former soldiers who married their wards. It's bound to happen in a society wracked with war for as long as ours was. Although the Vampyre kingdom is stuffy and traditional in a lot of ways, romance between a bodyguard and their ward has always been perfectly fine. Expected, even." Latimus grinned. "Lila and I were hoping this would happen when you volunteered to guard her, although we didn't expect it so quickly. Way to go, man. I could've taken some pointers from you when I was desperately in love with Lila for all those centuries."

Chuckling, Sam shrugged. "I've been smitten with her since your bonding ceremony, but every time I asked her out, she always suggested I bring Jack along."

"That's Glarys. She most likely convinced herself you were just being nice."

"She did, and I misread it as her not being interested in spending one-on-one time with me. I've never been all that great at reading women."

"Who is?" Latimus murmured. "Apologies go a long way. And flowers. I've learned a lot. Maybe I can teach you something now."

Breathing a laugh, Sam patted his upper arm. "I'll take any advice you have. I haven't taken a woman on a date in so long, I don't even remember the last time. What the hell do I do?"

Staring at the blue sky, eyes narrowed, Latimus contemplated. "Glarys is always doting on other people. I wonder how long it's been since she was doted upon. I'd say, take that angle. Find something that focuses on making her feel really special. And then there's wine. Lila loves wine, and she gets so adorably tipsy when I bring home a fancy bottle. Maybe it will work for you too."

"Duly noted," he said, giving a salute. "I can't wait to make her feel special. I've rarely met another person who's so thoughtful. The pasta and the freshly squeezed orange juice for Jack—that's just the beginning. She'd probably break her own back just to see any of your children smile. Hell, to see any of us smile."

"That she would. She's one in a million."

"Well, I appreciate you being on board with me taking the next step while I guard her." Sam extended his hand. "If you ever change your mind, let me know."

Shaking, Latimus grinned. "Make her happy, Sam. That's all I care about."

"Me too, Latimus. I swear."

When the training resumed and Sam returned to the kitchen, Glarys's sky-blue irises lit with joy.

"Oh, here," she said, urging him to sit at the kitchen island and placing a plate of steaming-hot appetizers in front of him. "I prepared this for you. I need a taste tester."

It was a good excuse, but Sam understood she'd made the plate for him as a gesture of affection. Taking a bite of the little puffy thing, he closed his eyes in ecstasy as he chewed.

"My god, woman. This is amazing. What is it?"

"Baked brie and spinach puff pastry." She was enchanting as she reveled in his obvious enjoyment. "I'm so glad you like it." Waiting for him to swallow, she asked, "How did it go with Latimus? Is he on board with us, um, you know...?"

"He's on board," Sam replied with a wink.

Her cheeks flushed, sending every drop of blood in his veins to his shaft. Goddess, she was so stunning.

"So should we go on a date?"

"I'm kind of traditional, here, Glarys, so if it's all right with you, I'd like to surprise you. Give me a few days so I can plan a proper date for us. Is that okay?"

"Yes," she said, eyes twinkling as she spoke in a gravelly voice. "That's very okay."

She got back to work, her gorgeous backside accentuated by her green dress, and Sam finished the succulent food, wondering when in the hell he'd become the luckiest man on the damn planet.

*Chapter 7*

The fundraiser at Takelia went well, as did Symon's birthday party the following day, and by the end of the week, Glarys was exhausted. She made sure to get a good night's sleep on Friday since Sam had informed her to be prepared to spend the entire day with him on Saturday. Excitement sparkled in his eyes as he told her to expect several surprises. It all seemed a bit silly to Glarys, who never wished for anyone to go out of their way for her, but she told herself to relax and enjoy being courted by a thoughtful, handsome suitor.

Sam had told her to dress casually Saturday morning but to pack a bag with nicer clothes and toiletries for later in the evening.

"Oh, is this an overnight thing?" she'd asked as she wiped the kitchen countertop Friday afternoon.

"Not unless you want it to be," he'd replied slyly. "You'll want to shower and refresh after our morning activities, and you'll have access to do so."

She'd given him a curious glare, wondering what in the heck she was in store for.

On Saturday morning, she stood in the kitchen dressed in yoga pants and a T-shirt, bag slung over her shoulder. Sam trailed in, black sweatpants clinging to his muscled legs, and she licked her lips in anticipation. Would she get to run her hands over the springy hairs beneath the fabric later?

"Ready?" he asked, fangs glowing as he grinned.

With a nod, they were on their way.

Sam drove them to a property on the outskirts of Astaria that looked rather fancy. As they parked, Glarys read the sign out front: **Astaria Day Spa and Resort**.

"A spa?" she asked, eyes wide. "I've never been to one."

"Didn't think you had since you spend all your time pampering everyone else. Today's about you, sweetie. Come on."

She took his extended hand, feeling a bit trepidatious. "I can't spend all day getting mollycoddled. This is too much—"

"Let me spoil you, honey," he said, squeezing her hand. "Please don't fight me on this. If you relax, you might just enjoy it," he said with a wink.

They entered the large front doors, and a butler awaited them with two glasses of champagne.

"Samwise, Son of Raythor," the butler said, handing him the glass before bowing to Glarys, "and Glarys, Daughter of Davel. So lovely to meet you both. I'm Artor and will be your host today."

"Oh, thank you," Glarys said, taking the glass and sipping. "This is lovely."

They followed Artor to a sitting room with plush couches, and a woman appeared dressed in fancy scrubs.

"Hello, Glarys. I'm Sana, your masseuse and facialist. I'm going to whisk you away with me while Sam takes care of some business."

"Business?" Glarys asked, arching a brow at Sam.

"No questions," he said, leaning down to kiss her on the forehead. "Have fun with Sana. I'll see you at the salt bath later."

*Salt bath?* Curious excitement flowed through her veins as she reveled in the touch of his firm lips. Sam followed Artor from the room, and she stood to address Sana.

"I don't know what I'm doing here."

"Looks like you're getting wooed," Sana said, her tone wistful. "How romantic. This way, please." Gesturing with her arm to the door, she stared expectantly at Glarys.

"Well, I guess I am," she muttered, following the nice lady through.

Three hours later, Glarys felt like a wet noodle. After the first massage of her life, Sana had given her a facial, which she thought might just be heaven on Earth. After showering in the expansive locker room shower to rid her body of the oil, she donned the bathing suit Sana had supplied and headed toward the spa area. There were several rooms with private whirlpools and salt baths, and Sana led her to one, her eyes twinkling.

"Have fun," the kind lady said before swinging open the door.

She noticed Sam standing by the salt pool, green smoothie in hand, clad only in swim shorts. The muscles of his abdomen formed a firm six-pack under springy brown hair, and saliva pooled in her throat. Approaching him, she asked, "Is that for me?"

"Yep," he said, handing her the smoothie. "That's lunch. I have a surprise for dinner later. But for now, I'm going to hang in the pool with you—if you're okay with that."

Nodding, she slipped her hand in his, and he led her into the salt pool. She caught him up on her amazing morning, unable to believe he was treating her to such splendor. Eventually, they moved to the steaming whirlpool, Sam scooching beside her and placing his arm over her shoulders as the jets pounded their upper backs.

"Goddess, this feels heavenly," she said, eyes closed as her head rested on his arm. "How am I going to go back to regular life? You've ruined me."

Chuckling, he rested his head against hers. "I figure you deserve pampering more than anyone, Glarys. You're so damn thoughtful."

"I think you might have surpassed me," she said, snuggling into his side, not even caring that her love handle was brushing against his perfect abdomen. Who had the energy to care when they felt so fantastic?

"Oh, there's more to come—just wait."

Lifting her lids, she smiled up at him. "Thank you. Just in case I forget to say it later."

"You're welcome." His wet fingers combed through the hair at her temple. "I mean, I should be thanking you. All that soft, wet skin against me. You're absolutely gorgeous, Glarys."

Tears pricked her eyes as emotion overcame her. "Sam," she whispered.

"Don't cry, honey," he said, concern filtering over his strong features.

"They're happy tears. You've made me so happy today."

His lips curved as her heart thrummed. "Good." Placing a poignant kiss on her lips, he asked, "Are you ready for the next part of our day?"

"I'm not sure I can take any more, but why not?"

He led her from the spa room, and Sana met them outside. She directed Glarys to shower again before taking her to the styling room. A professional stylist blew out her hair while a makeup artist applied some cosmetics, although Glarys told her to keep it natural. Glancing at her watch, she realized it was almost dinnertime.

Artor met her outside the locker room and led her through the spa to an outdoor patio. A table was set for two overlooking the meadow, two candles burning atop the white tablecloth.

"My lady," Sam said, appearing and offering her his arm. After she was seated, he sat across from her, looking rather nervous.

"What are you up to?"

"So while you were getting pampered today, I spent hours preparing tonight's meal. I'm an okay cook but have always wanted to get better. I hired the chef to teach me and prepped and cooked everything we're having tonight. I felt like someone should cook for you for once."

"How thoughtful," she said, overcome by the gesture.

"Don't say that yet. Let's see how it tastes, and then we'll assess."

Chuckling, she sampled the white wine the server poured, noting it was excellent, and settled in for the first course.

She and Sam made easy conversation, getting to know each other better as she savored the food. The arugula salad with walnuts and gorgonzola was fantastic, but the main course was excellent.

"Glazed salmon with gnocchi and steamed vegetables," the chef said, setting the plates in front of them. "Your husband here worked really hard to plan the menu and prepare the dishes with me, ma'am."

"I love salmon," she said, winking at Sam in reference to the chef calling him her "husband."

"Lila told me." Red splotches appeared on his cheeks, causing her body to enflame with heat. "And she said you like cannoli too. Those are next."

"Oh, my. I'm going to gain a hundred pounds. Thank you, Chef," she said to the man before he politely nodded and walked away. Gazing at Sam, she said in a gravelly voice, "And thank you, Sam. I don't know what to say."

"Less talk, more eat," he teased, lifting his fork. "Dig in."

Several glasses of wine and a full belly later, she placed her hands over her abdomen and sat back, expelling a huge breath. "That's it. I'm never eating again. Vampyres aren't supposed to like food anyway, but that was absolutely amazing."

"I'm so glad you enjoyed it." Twirling the wine in his glass, Sam's gaze was hooded. "I hope you've had a good day, honey."

"So good," she said, overwhelmed with gratitude. "You might have shot yourself in the foot. Not sure how you're going to top this for our next date."

Chuckling, he sipped his wine. "I'll find something up my sleeve."

He drove them home, Glarys content and sated as she sat beside him. When they entered the darkened castle, he began trailing to the kitchen, but she grabbed his wrist and tugged him toward the large staircase.

Brown irises studied her as he hesitated. "I didn't do all this to make you feel obligated to me, Glarys. I'm okay just watching a movie and holding you...and maybe kissing you a few hundred times." He grinned, giving a playful shrug. "I'm not sure what pace you prefer, but any pace is fine with me as long as you look at me with those pretty eyes."

Closing the distance between them, she palmed his cheeks. "There hasn't really been any pace since my husband died. I was so sure I'd never be held by someone again. Time is precious, and I don't want to squander it. If you want me, I'd really like to make love to you, Sam. Does that make me a hussy?" She giggled.

Sliding his arm around her waist, he aligned their bodies, nuzzling her nose with his. "If it does, I'm here for it. Are you sure, honey?"

Nodding, she bit her lip, loving the desire that flared in his eyes. "I'm sure."

"Put your arms around my neck," he all but growled.

Complying, she held tight as he slid his arm under her knees and lifted her.

"Remember, I'm carrying extra weight from that amazing dinner. Don't strain yourself."

Charging up the stairs with her against his body, he said, "Well, let's burn those calories off, sweetheart."

Sighing, she figured making love to Sam would probably be the best form of exercise ever invented. Heart pounding in anticipation, she placed fervent kisses on his neck as he crossed the threshold to her room, closing the door behind him.

S am placed Glarys atop the bed, marveling at her snow-white hair and smiling face as she stared back at him. Whatever the stylists had done made her look stunning. He couldn't decide whether he liked her more like this—all gussied up—or makeup-free and half-naked in the plain swimsuit she wore at the spa. Thrilled he didn't have to choose, he lowered above her, balancing on his arm before settling most of the weight on his hip. Sprawling over her, he devoured her mouth, loving the little shrieks of pleasure she mewled down his throat.

He wanted to rip her clothes off and plunge into her quaking body, but he told himself to go slow. Only having one arm precluded him from being able to ravish her as extensively as he wanted, but he'd focus every ounce of energy from his good arm to make her scream. Palming his pecs, she gently pressed, urging him to break the kiss.

"I love kissing you," she said, breathless. "But I need to feel you against me. Let me take this dress off."

Sitting up, he pulled her to stand, leaning back on his arm as she unclasped the two front buttons and slid the dress over her head, tossing it over the nearby chair. Clad in her white bra and panties, Sam gazed at her beauty. Thick, succulent thighs led to full calves and those adorable toes. Her waist curved with hollows he craved to explore with his tongue. Full breasts heaved as she stared down at him.

"I wish I could unclasp your bra, but I can't," he said, lifting his one hand, slightly discomfited. "Can you do it?"

Gaze cemented to his, she reached behind and unfastened the bra, tossing it to lie with the dress. "Do you want me to take my underwear off too?"

"Come here," he said, crooking his finger at her. "I can definitely manage that."

She stepped forward, and he hooked his fingers inside the cotton material, dragging it down until she stepped out of it. Hurling it toward the chair, he grinned at her soft chuckle.

"Are you eager, Sam?"

"So fucking eager," he murmured, gliding his arm around her waist and drawing her toward him. Resting his forehead beneath her breasts, he inhaled her lavender scent as she whispered his name. Placing a soft kiss on her stomach, he smelled her resulting gush of arousal as the skin quivered beneath his lips.

Vampyres had heightened senses for arousal, and hers was intoxicating.

Standing, he reached behind and grabbed a fistful of his shirt, pulling it over his head. His belt and pants were next. After centuries of learning to function with one hand, he knew how to remove them, but she placed her hand over his, stilling him.

"Let me."

Nodding, he proceeded to watch her unbuckle his belt and slide it off before slowly unfastening his pants. Kicking off his shoes, he shimmied everything to the ground, including his boxer briefs, and kicked them away.

Naked, he gazed at her as she stared at his engorged cock.

Encircling it with her fingers, she lightly squeezed as he gritted his teeth, determined to let her explore at her own pace.

"My god, it's been so long since I've touched one of these..." Biting her lip, she looked up at him and ran her thumb over the mushroom-shaped head, spreading the tiny wet droplet over the aching skin. "I hope I don't disappoint you."

"Honey, you've already made every dream I've ever had come true. Look at that pretty hand around my cock." Jutting into her palm, he growled. "Goddess, I want you so much."

Wrinkling her nose, she asked, "Are hands pretty? I've never thought of them that way."

Done with conversation, he slid his arm around her waist and tugged her to bed, gently urging her to lie across the comforter. "Yours are," he said, crawling over her. "Just like every other part of you." Lowering his lips to hers, he plunged his tongue inside her mouth, desperate to taste her again.

As he kissed her, he trailed his hand over her breast, running his thumb over her nipple and tweaking it with his fingers. She moaned beneath him, her body writhing against him, and he ached with gratitude that she would let him love her this way. Trailing kisses over her neck toward her breast, he sucked the nipple between his lips, lathering her with his saliva, wanting to mark her with his scent. Thin fingers thrust into his hair, the tugging sensation driving him insane with lust.

Once her nipple was puckered and tight, he kissed his way to the other, lavishing it with the same attention until it stood pointed and ready. Sliding his hand to the juncture of her thighs, he cupped her mound, the prickly hairs scratching his palm.

"I want to kiss you here," he said, flexing his hand, "but I think I might explode if I don't get inside you, honey."

"You can kiss me there next time," she said, tugging his hair so he rose above her. "And I might just kiss you down there too."

He groaned, moving his body into position as the erotic thought of her mouth around his stiff cock blazed in his mind.

"Do you want me to use a condom?"

Although Vampyres couldn't transmit disease through intercourse due to their self-healing bodies, there was still the chance of pregnancy.

Her expression grew somber. "No. I went through my change after menopause, so I can't get pregnant anymore."

Hating that he'd brought up something that seemed to make her sad, he cupped her face. "I'm sorry."

"Don't be," she said, covering his lips with her fingers. "Please, Sam. I need you. Make love to me."

Balancing on the stub of his arm and his side, he glided his hand between her silky legs and pushed her thigh open. Probing, he found her swollen folds with the head of his shaft, nudging until he was seated at her wet opening. Gaze cemented to hers, he began to push inside.

"Oh, yes," she cried, lips wet from his previous kisses, looking like a goddess beneath him. "I feel you *everywhere*."

"Glarys," he gritted, pushing inside her, inch by inch. "You feel so good, sweetheart. All slick and hot. Damn, honey." Settling over her, he lifted her leg across his back before placing his palm on the comforter beside her head. Resting his weight on his good arm, he began to undulate his hips, hissing tight breaths as her silken channel squeezed his sensitive skin.

She wrapped her arms around him, pulling him close, as her leg pushed against his ass. Urged on by her excited mewls, he plunged into her, over and over, understanding this must be what one experienced in the Passage. Pure, unadulterated bliss. Merging his lips with hers, he kissed her thoroughly and deeply as he loved her, striving to reach a place inside that drove her wild.

Frustrated he only had one hand, he wondered if he should stimulate the little nub hidden in her folds as he loved her, knowing some women needed that extra stimulation to reach orgasm. Oh, how he'd love to balance above her and hammer into her while circling the tiny bud, but his injury made that impossible.

Shifting his hips, he changed the angle, hoping to rub against the sensitive spot with the base of his shaft while he plunged deep inside. It must've worked because she gasped, lids flying open as her mouth fell agape.

"Yes! Like that. Oh, Sam, please don't stop. That's perfect."

"Like this?" he asked, increasing the pace of his hips, struggling to breathe but desperate to make her come.

"Mm-hmm..." Her short hair fanned over the mattress as she nodded, those sexy fangs squishing the flesh of her bottom lip. "Just like that. Oh, god..."

As focused as he'd ever been, he gyrated into her, feeling his balls constrict as her body tightened. Her taut channel gripped his cock as she began to come, head thrown back as she cried his name. He pumped into her, his lungs spasming, desperate for air, before he closed his eyes and released the orgasm. Milky jets spurted from his jolting shaft, coating her deepest place as he claimed her. Collapsing atop her trembling body, they gulped air into their heaving chests until she began to giggle.

"*Ohmygod*," she breathed, the words jumbled together as she ran her fingernails over his sweaty back, causing his body to lurch against her with pleasure. "Sam...that was...oh, my..."

"Nothing has ever felt so good," he murmured into her neck, limp and sated. "I think your gorgeous body was made for me, honey."

"I'm so happy you think I'm pretty," she said, emotion in her voice.

Lifting his head, he stroked the tear that escaped her eye. "Sweetheart?"

"I just haven't felt pretty in so long. I felt old and unwanted and convinced myself that was okay because I had the kids around. But you would look at me and tell me such nice things." She stroked his jaw, her gaze reverent. "It means so much, Sam. I'm incredibly lucky to be with you. You could have any woman you set your sights on."

"I don't want any woman but you," he said, the statement true on every level. "I think you're magnificent. And you don't seem to mind that I'm not quite whole." His gaze trailed to his stub before returning to her.

"You're whole in every way." Lifting her head, she placed a poignant kiss on the stub of his arm, causing a pang in his solar plexus. It was an acceptance of something he'd been ashamed of for centuries before finally learning to bear it, and he felt his own eyes well with moisture.

"Thank you," he whispered, lowering to kiss her. "I wish I had two hands to touch you twice as often, but I'll do my best with the one I've got."

"Your best is amazing. I feel like I could sleep for twenty years after the pampering and fantastic sex. You made my decade, for sure."

Chuckling, he planted one last kiss on her lips before pushing away and sliding from her body. Striding to the bathroom, he grabbed a cloth and returned, wiping away his release while her cheeks glowed red. After tossing it on the bathroom counter, Sam found Glarys turning back the covers. Rubbing the back of his neck, he wondered if he should ask to sleep with her. He'd love nothing more than to cuddle but didn't want to impose.

"Well?" she said, extending her arms as she sat with her back against the pillows. Her breasts called to him, still flushed and full as she stared at him expectantly.

"You're not going to love me and leave me, are you?"

Laughing, he inched closer. "I don't want you to feel obligated to sleep with me. I know some people like their privacy."

Her lips formed a frown. "I mean, I'd really like you to hold me, but if that's not your thing, that's okay. I like snuggling. Always have."

Feeling himself beam, he crawled into bed and pulled her to his side, loving how she wiggled against him. "I like snuggling too. Especially with you."

"Good night," she said, yawning as she rested her cheek on his chest. "Feel free to wake me up in a few hours and do that to me again, okay?"

Breathing a laugh, he stroked her hair as she relaxed against him. "Count on it, honey. Now that I've loved you once, I don't think I'll be able to stop."

"Thank the goddess," she mumbled into his skin.

Closing his eyes, he sent a prayer of thanks to Etherya. Wrapped in his woman's luscious scent, he succumbed to slumber.

# Chapter 8

They fell into a cozy pattern, and Sam reveled in how comfortable he was around Glarys. He'd always been somewhat of a loner, preferring solitude and quiet, but spending time with her was amazing. He would accompany her as she buzzed about the kingdom spearheading parties for wealthy aristocrats and the royal children. Although the functions were quite different, she poured just as much energy into the children's fetes as she did the stuffy royal soirees. For someone who insisted she was past her prime, the woman had a plethora of infectious energy.

Sam had never craved companionship but now understood how magnificent a relationship could be if one found the right person. As the months wore on and their relationship flourished, Sam became increasingly convinced Glarys was the one.

One night, as they sat on the couch watching The Hunger Games, he lifted the remote and paused the movie.

"Do you need more popcorn?" she asked, peering over at the empty bowl.

"No," he said, turning to face her and taking her hand in his. "I'd like to talk to you about something and can't decide on the right time, so I figure it's best to just blurt it out."

"Okay," she said, eyes growing wide. "What is it?"

Swallowing thickly, he rubbed her hand with his thumb. "I really enjoy spending time with you, Glarys."

Those plush pink lips curved into a smile. "I love spending time with you too. Even when you snore against my neck when we're sleeping."

Chuckling, he shook his head. "Never kept anyone around long enough to tell me whether I snore or not. I sure am sorry it's so loud."

"You know I'm only teasing," she said, swatting his chest. "I love having you close to me, so it's a small price to pay."

Feeling his eyes dart between hers, he tamped down his nervousness. "Are you open to bonding with someone again?"

Her shoulders straightened as surprise washed over her features.

"Because I sure would like to ask you to bond with me. I'll do it right and make it all formal, but I figured it's best to ask you first and make sure you'll say yes."

Exhaling a slow breath, she palmed his cheek. "Sam," she said, her voice raspy. "That's so lovely for you to say..."

"But?"

"Well..." Her fangs toyed with her lip as she contemplated. "I can't have children of my own anymore and feel like it would be selfish to tie you to me. Don't you want children one day? What if you wake up centuries from now and realize you're bound to someone who can't give you what you need?"

Eyes narrowed, he stared at the ceiling as he pondered. "I've never had a hankerin' for kids like some people do. When Jack lived with me after my sister passed, I didn't mind raising him but didn't feel like I was giving him everything he needed. That's why I asked Lila to adopt him. That woman was born to be a mother."

Chuckling, Glarys nodded. "She certainly was."

"I've always functioned pretty well on my own and never really craved kids or a family. Until you. Now, I see myself wanting to bond with you and build a future together. If we decide we want kids down the road, we could always adopt. I mean, what are your thoughts on kids?"

"I've always been so consumed with the royal children, and now their children, they've filled any void I might've had from not having my own kids. As long as they're around, I don't think I'll want to have children down the road. If that changes, I'd be open to adoption. Still, I want you to think this through, Sam. I don't want to deny you anything."

"Deny me?" he asked, incredulous. "Goddess, Glarys, you're gorgeous and caring and so much smarter than me. Hell, I bet you've read every book in this room," he said, gesturing to the bookshelves overflowing with human and Vampyre manuscripts. "I can barely read the books Symon and Adelyn bring home from school when we visit Lila and Latimus. Sometimes, I speak and wonder if I conjured the words right and hope you're not internally laughing at me."

She pursed her lips, laughter in her ice-blue eyes.

"What?"

"It's conjugate, not conjure, and I'm only laughing because you're so adorable right now."

"See?" he asked, playfully rolling his eyes. "I don't even know the difference."

"If you think for one second I give a fig about that, you still don't know me." Sliding her arms around his neck, she rubbed her nose against his. "I couldn't care less if you can't read a damn word.

You're a skillful soldier who does everything in his power to ensure my safety. When I think about all the places and functions I drag you to—and you've never complained, not once. Talk about patient and kind... You're wonderful, Sam, and I'm so enamored with the way you speak. It's quite endearing and makes my knees week every damn time."

"Yeah?" he asked, brushing her lips with his.

Nodding, she tugged him closer. "I *really* like it when you whisper in my ear while we're making love."

Overcome with desire for her, he joined his lips to hers as he pressed her back into the couch. Loving her resulting giggle, he proceeded to speak a multitude of words in her ear—some dirty, and some unintelligible—as he made love to her.

Once they were sated and struggling to catch their breath as they lay entwined on the couch, she playfully nipped his jaw.

"Well, in case you haven't figured it out, if you're okay bonding with someone who can't have kids, I'll say yes, Sam."

Thrilled to his core, he hugged her close. "Okay, let me think of something real special, honey. You deserve that."

"All I want is you," she mumbled against his skin.

Replete and happy, he closed his eyes and relaxed into her sweat-soaked body as they recovered.

## Chapter 9

Sam set about planning the perfect proposal for Glarys as he continued to protect her. Using a large chunk of the cash he had saved from his previous private security job, he visited the jeweler in the main square and bought her an expensive ring. It was a diamond surrounded by tiny sapphires that matched her eyes. Hoping like hell she'd think it was as pretty as he did, he handed over the cash once the jeweler had boxed it up.

"Congratulations on your upcoming nuptials, sir," he said with a smile. "I wish you all the best."

"Thanks," he said, holding the box high as he shrugged. "I've just got to get her to say yes."

"Well, that ring is one of our finest. I'm sure she'll appreciate it."

"Hope so," Sam said, giving him a friendly salute before heading back to the castle.

Glarys was flitting around the kitchen as always, and he hid the ring in the dresser in Heden's old room, content she wouldn't find it. He planned to take her on a romantic picnic by the river next week and would propose to her there.

Already nervous, he entered the kitchen, his heart skipping a beat as her eyes twinkled with ever-present fondness for him. They hadn't said the "L" word yet, but he certainly was in love with her, deep in his bones and to the tip of his toes. Hopefully, once he proposed and professed his love, she'd reciprocate in kind.

"There's my handsome bodyguard," she said, wrapping an arm around his neck and placing a wet kiss on his cheek. "Did you get everything you needed in town?"

Mischief sparkled in her eyes as he realized she was onto him.

"Yup," he said, running his hand through his hair. "Got the same haircut I always get."

"It looks sexy." She waggled her eyebrows. "Is that all you got in town? A haircut?"

"Yes, ma'am."

"Mm-hmm..." Eyes narrowing, she playfully swatted him before backing away. "The meal is almost done for family dinner tonight, and everyone should be here soon. Want to set the table?"

"Sure." Making himself useful, he helped his woman, inwardly chuckling at how perceptive she was. Life with her would always keep him on his toes, and damn if that didn't make him a hundred shades of excited.

Consumed with thoughts of their upcoming centuries together, he set the table in the exact way she'd shown him, feeling proud of himself when she complimented him. Hell, he might even become fancy with a little help from her. Leaning down, he drew her into a breathless kiss where they stood by the set table.

"Oh, my," she said, bringing her fingers to her lips. "What was that for?"

"For teaching me new things. It's one of the things I love most about you, honey."

Her resulting smile all but melted his heart. "Thank you. I love learning from you too."

"What have you learned from me?" he asked softly.

Cupping his face, she whispered, "How to love again."

Overcome with feeling for her, he pulled her close and held her in a passionate embrace until the pitter-patter of tiny feet interrupted them, and they eventually sat down for dinner.

A few days later, Glarys was running late, which was unusual for her structured schedule. Placing her supplies and baked goods in the bags upon the counter, she dropped a container and uttered a curse.

"Hey," Sam said, swooping in and picking it up as she struggled to temper her frustration. "You okay, honey?"

"I'm never late, but I forgot Miranda asked me to make deviled eggs. They're her favorite. Thank the goddess I had some extra boiled eggs in the fridge, but it set me behind this morning."

"That's okay. I can drive us in the four-wheeler so we don't have to rush to the train."

Feeling her shoulders relax, she inhaled a few deep breaths. "Are you sure?"

"Of course. It's a nice day, and I could use some sun. Take your time—we'll head out whenever you're ready. I'm going to go to the barracks and grab a knife to stick in my boot, just in case."

Worry washed over Glarys. "Latimus told me about the attack last week outside Uteria. Will we be safe?"

"I won't let anything happen to you, honey. It's always good to have a backup in case your firearm gets knocked away." His hand curved over her shoulder. "Let me put that salary Latimus is paying me to use, okay? I've got you."

The words rang true as she'd never felt safer with anyone than she did with Sam. "Okay, let me get everything together." She shooed him away as she resumed packing everything. "I'll be ready in five minutes."

Once he was armed with his glock and a knife in his boot and the four-wheeler had been loaded, they headed through the meadow and eventually through Etherya's protective wall. As they drove along the open fields to Uteria, Glarys was overcome with love for her strong, thoughtful Vampyre. She knew he was close to proposing, and she was ready to profess those three magic words to him. Once they returned to Astaria that evening, she would hold him tight as he moved inside her deepest place and whisper the words while she stared into those deep brown eyes. Shivering in anticipation, she could barely contain her grin.

Suddenly, a shrill yell sounded to her right, audible above the engine of the four-wheeler, and she realized they were being attacked. Deamons seemed to appear from every angle as they charged the car, causing Sam to bring it to a grinding halt.

"Stay in the car," he ordered before exiting the vehicle. Pulling the gun from his holster, he shot a Deamon directly in the eyes before another grabbed Sam's arm, whirling him around and then landing a solid punch on his face.

Sam grunted and shot the creature in the abdomen, spinning to kick another in his side. As that Deamon fell to the ground, he shot two more approaching from the rear between the eyes. Pivoting around to where the last Deamon lay gasping for breath on the ground, Sam aimed his gun and released the bullet into the monster's brain.

Chest heaving from the exertion of fighting five Deamons, Sam held up his hand. "Stay there, honey. Let me assess."

Glarys admired his prowess as he inspected the area around the car. Never had she seen someone fight off five assailants so effectively. Marveling at his skill, she truly understood what a magnificent warrior he was. Grateful for his fervent protection, she waited.

"I think they're all dead," he said, still clutching the gun, as his gaze roved over the slain bodies.

Suddenly, a Vampyre appeared in front of the four-wheeler, materializing from thin air, and Glarys gasped. As he came into sight, she noticed his resemblance to Latimus and understood this was Bakari, the lost Vampyre royal sibling, and their newest foe.

Sam lifted the gun, aiming it at the man's chest.

Bakari gave a sinister chuckle, shaking his head as Sam stood firm. "You know my self-healing abilities are vast considering I have the pure blood of the Vampyre king and queen flowing through my veins, Samwise. It's pointless to shoot me."

Surreptitiously reaching into her purse, Glarys dialed Latimus, leaving the line open so he would hopefully hear the conversation. Clicking the volume button so his voice wouldn't boom, she heard him answer and closed her eyes in relief.

"Your girlfriend just called my brother, Sam, and I'd really like to punish her for that, so you're going to need to get out of my way. I can kill you, or you can step aside. Your choice."

"Glarys and I don't want no trouble," Sam said, legs spread wide as he stood immobile. "We have no part in the vengeance you seek."

"I'm not sure that's true. Glarys was there when I was born, yet she never noticed I was mercilessly whisked away by the traitorous soothsayers to a world that wasn't mine."

"I'm so sorry for what happened to you, son," Glarys said, shaking her head as she trembled in the seat. "I had no idea what occurred all those centuries ago. If I did, I would've done my best to help you."

"Lies," Bakari gritted through his teeth. "You all lie and have damned me to be an outcast from the realm in which I should thrive. In return, I will decimate each one of you and rule in perpetuity, showcasing my true heritage. My siblings' affinity toward you makes you an excellent target, Glarys."

Glarys felt such overwhelming sympathy for him. Yes, it was a strange sentiment being that he was threatening their lives, but she felt it all the same. Wishing she could travel centuries into the past and rewrite his tragic history, she waited, hoping Latimus had figured out by now that they were under attack.

Lifting a sword from his back, Bakari held it high. "It's poison-tipped, Sam. Don't make me cut off your other arm. Somehow, I think that would be worse than dying for you."

Neither budged until Bakari began to step forward.

"Out of my way, peasant."

Sam charged, lunging out of the way when Bakari sliced the sword through the air. Rotating, he swiped Bakari's legs with one of his own, causing the massive Vampyre to lose his balance and fall to the ground. Scrambling, Sam stood and whirled, appearing to contemplate the best place to lodge a bullet in Bakari's self-healing body. If Sam hit the right spot, he could temporarily maim him and hopefully restrain him while they waited for backup.

As Sam faced his foe, Glarys marveled at how quickly Bakari jumped to his feet. His muscular arms held the sword high as Sam pulled the trigger, releasing the bullet at the same time the hulking Vampyre sliced the blade through his arm.

Glarys screamed, noting the blood that began to spurt from the wound as Sam's severed arm lay on the ground.

Bakari rushed her, and she closed her eyes, praying to Etherya for a quick death. Suddenly, Bakari gasped and gripped his neck. Blood pumped through his fingers, and he pivoted.

"One more move, and I'll use the eight-shooter instead of the gun, asshole," Latimus said from behind. "I don't want to kill my own brother, but you're making it really hard, Bakari."

"Let this be a lesson that I will come after everyone you love," Bakari spat, "even this old hag. Until we meet again, *brother.*" Closing his eyes, he dematerialized.

"Are you okay?" Latimus asked, rushing toward her.

"Yes," she said, climbing from the vehicle and rushing to Sam, who now sat on the grass staring at his bleeding arm where it rested several feet away.

"Evie transported me here and should be back any minute with Nolan."

Nodding, Glarys crouched beside Sam. "Hold on, sweetheart," she said, pulling her scarf from her purse and holding it to his wound.

"I'm sorry I didn't protect you better," he said, appearing utterly defeated.

"You were amazing." She placed a kiss on his lips and cupped his jaw. "Thank you, Sam."

Nolan appeared with Evie and rushed to Sam's side. "The blade was poisoned?" he asked.

"Yes," Sam said.

"Okay. Glarys, please wrap the limb in that scarf."

She rushed to follow his directive, attempting to be careful. Taking the limb, Evie hugged Sam close.

"Hold on," Evie said, closing her eyes. "Sadie's waiting for us at the infirmary. Let's go." With a whoosh, she and Sam disappeared.

"Will you and Sadie be able to reattach the arm?" Glarys asked softly.

"I don't know," Nolan said. "It depends on the amount of damage."

"Oh, my," Glarys said, tears forming in her eyes. "He was already frustrated that he'd lost one arm. I hope you can repair the other."

"If we can't, we can certainly work to make a functioning prosthetic. There have been many advancements in the human world with prosthetics, and losing multiple limbs isn't nearly the challenge it used to be."

"I hope not," Glarys said, knowing the loss would be emotionally devastating to Sam. Determined to help him through it, she lifted her chin. "I need to be by his side. Can one of you call Evie to transport me?"

"I'm on it, Glarys," Evie said, appearing beside her. "Come on, put your arms around my neck."

Listening to the Slayer-Deamon, she followed her command and closed her eyes as the woman transported her to the infirmary at Uteria.

# Chapter 10

S am awoke feeling groggy. He licked the roof of his mouth. It tasted awful, and his throat was so dry the air scratched his windpipe. Struggling to clear his throat, he glanced down at his left arm, the stub slightly protruding. Gazing to his right arm, he saw the white bindings, so pristine as they covered his now-severed limb.

Resting his head back on the pillow, he wanted to weep for everything he'd lost but realized tears wouldn't ease the pain. Nothing could. He was now as useless as a shot of whiskey in a dry town.

Overwhelmed with emotion, he struggled to regulate his breathing as he felt a presence beside him.

"You're awake," Glarys's sweet voice said, nearing his ear as she plopped down in the chair beside the bed. "Thank the goddess. How are you feeling?"

Swallowing, he gazed into those gorgeous eyes, understanding it would be one of the last times. No way in hell would he let her waste her future on an armless man with no means to protect her. Feeling utterly defeated, he turned his head and focused on the ceiling, unable to bear the pity in her ice-blue irises.

"I'm fine," he said tersely.

She was silent a moment before reaching to cup his jaw. "Sam—"

"No," he said, shaking her hand away. "I don't want you to see me like this, Glarys."

"Like what?" she asked, anger infusing her tone. "Like the man who valiantly protected me and ensured my safety?"

Clenching his lids, he tried to will her away. "I'm not doing this now, while I'm lying here like an invalid."

"Sam…"

"Please, Glarys. If you care for me at all, you'll give me some space." He could see her chin quivering out of the corner of his eye and hated himself for hurting her, but he just couldn't handle being near her, surrounded by her scent and ethereal beauty. They reminded him of things he'd never deserve now that he'd truly lost everything.

Thankfully, they were saved from the awkward moment by Nolan, who entered the room with a kind smile under his short chestnut brown hair.

"Good morning, Sam. Glad to see you're awake. I'd like to update you on your prognosis and options moving forward. Glarys is certainly welcome to stay if you'd like."

"Actually, I'd rather talk alone, doc," Sam said, agony wracking his frame at the look of pain that shot across Glarys's face.

"Well, then," she said, standing and holding her hand over her heart as if to hold it together while it broke in her chest, "I'll leave you to it. I'll come back to check on Sam later." All but fleeing from the room, she left her lavender scent behind, flooding his nostrils.

"Sam," Nolan said, sliding into Glarys's chair. "I understand this is a huge shock, but losing a limb isn't the tragedy it used to be. Humans have made so many advancements recently. I've studied them closely and am ready to help fit you with a prosthesis."

"So it's gone for good?"

Nolan gave a slow nod. "Yes. I tried to reattach the arm but was unable to render it effective. After several hours of surgery, Sadie and I couldn't see a way to save it. The limb was severed above the elbow. I'm so very sorry, Sam."

"Well, that gives me a few more inches on that side than this one, I guess," he said, gesturing with his head toward his left stub.

"Both of your arms are eligible for a new type of prosthetic called a Modular Prosthetic Limb or MPL. It's capable of interpreting and converting signals from the body's nervous system and channeling them into motion."

Sam contemplated, thinking it all sounded a bit too futuristic and plastic for his taste. "Can I feel through the fake arms?"

"The fingers are equipped with over one hundred sensors that detect sensations such as force, contact, and temperature. It's not perfect, but it does allow for tactile feedback. I postulate it will restore ninety percent of your arm function."

"But I'd always look like a damn robot," he said, frustrated. "And how would I ever hold or touch someone again?" he asked, thinking of Glarys. "It all seems phooey to me."

"Well, you don't have to make any decisions now. You've been through a hell of an ordeal, Sam. Let's get that wound healed and back to one hundred percent, and then we can discuss options."

"Thanks, doc. I appreciate you trying so hard to save it."

"You're welcome." Standing, Nolan contemplated him. "Glarys has been here since the second you arrived, Sam. It's obvious she's deeply in love with you. I hope you let her support you through this."

"She's in love with someone strong who strived to protect her, not the man I am now."

"You're still strong, Sam," Nolan said, sliding a hand over his shoulder. "This injury hasn't changed one bit of your inner fortitude or kindness. Sadie is an expert in human psychology and PTSD, and I hope you'll sit down to talk with her. She's available anytime you're ready. All of us want to support you through this."

"Thanks." Feeling exhausted, Sam observed Nolan leave the room and tried like hell not to focus on the fact he wished Bakari had killed him in the meadow instead of rendering him inept and hopeless.

# Chapter 11

G larys threw herself into her work, cleaning every inch of the mansion as if her life depended on it. Perhaps it did, since her heart had devolved into a heap of broken mush. After she left Sam a week ago, he'd refused to see her when she returned to the infirmary. Sadie, the kind physician and Nolan's wife, had hugged her as she burst into tears.

"It's a devastating loss, Glarys," she'd said, rubbing her back in a soothing gesture. "He's got to come to terms with it in his own way. You'll know when he's ready to see you."

"What if he's never ready?" she asked, sniffling into the wadded tissue she pulled from her purse. "Doesn't he understand I don't give a fig about his arm?"

"He's as stubborn as you are. Give him some time. I promise, it will work out."

Glarys had left the kind doctor and returned home, wondering how her life had devolved to this level of extreme despair. She missed Sam so desperately that she would cry into her pillow each night, craving his gentle snores and loving caresses. Perhaps that was why he was pushing her away: he felt his inability to touch her would preclude her from loving him back. Nothing could be further from the truth. Glarys longed to wrap her arms around him and show him they could still maintain their fervent and passionate connection. If only he understood how much she craved his presence; how vehemently she missed his sweet kisses.

A few days after the attack, Sadie informed her Sam had moved into one of the vacant cabins at the edge of Uteria. She and Nolan checked on him daily, making sure he was stocked with Slayer blood and ensuring he drank it. Although he was stubborn, he was reluctantly imbibing enough to stay alive.

Glarys debated the best way to approach him since he was still adamant he didn't want to see her. The sentiment stung. She ached to comfort him and help him heal—not just from the wound, but from the emotional scars it had invoked.

A week after his injury, as she cleaned Heden's room, furiously wiping down every speck of the vacant chamber, the anger that had been welling burned inside her gut. Opening the dresser drawer to dust inside, she gasped when she saw the black bag. Pulling it open, she clutched the felt box inside. With shaking fingers, she opened it to reveal a magnificent ring.

Tears flooded her eyes as she realized Sam had hidden it so she wouldn't find it before he proposed.

Closing the box, she tightened her fist around it, squeezing for dear life. Unwilling to let him push her away any longer, she rushed to her chamber to shower and then called Latimus.

"Hey, Glarys," his deep voice answered. "You okay?"

"I need you to pick me up and drive me to the cabin Sam's staying in at Uteria. You know I wouldn't ask you to interrupt your day if it wasn't important, but I need to speak with him, and I'm done letting him push me away."

She could almost feel his smile through the phone. "I'll be there in twenty-five minutes."

Over an hour later, she felt a crack in her resolve as they pulled up to the remote cabin on the outskirts of Uteria. Steeling herself, she exited the vehicle and straightened her shoulders, silently staring at the wooden shack.

"You can do this, Glarys," Latimus said from behind the wheel. "I'll be at the barracks behind the castle if you need me. Call anytime. Good luck." With a salute, he drove away.

Inhaling a deep breath, she climbed the creaky stairs and knocked on the door. Answered by nothing but resounding silence, she began to pound until she heard, "For the goddess's sake, come in before you beat the door down!"

Pushing it open, she headed inside, noting the dimness of the small cabin. Sam sat on the bed with his back against the headboard, long legs stretched in front of him, bare feet crossed at the ankles. He only wore sweatpants, that gorgeous abdomen making her mouth water. God, but she'd missed the sight of his smooth skin.

Planting her fists on her hips, she tapped her foot. "Well? You don't remember how to return a phone call?"

Sighing, he pressed his head against the headboard. "In case you haven't noticed, I can't really work a phone these days."

With a *harrumph*, she closed the cabin door and proceeded to open the curtains, causing beams of sunlight to blanket the room.

"Hey!" he said, squinting. "I wanted those closed."

"Well, too bad," she said, suddenly furious he'd all but given up. Where was the strong, steady soldier she fell in love with? "I'm pretty disappointed in you, Sam, and mad as hell that you're pushing me away."

"What do you want me to say, Glarys?" His tone was devoid of emotion, sending a jolt of fear down her spine. "It's over for me."

"Oh, holy hell." Stomping over to him, she gripped his shoulder and tugged. "Stand up."

He glared at her. "What are you doing, woman—?"

"I know you still have perfectly functioning legs, so I want you to stand the hell up, Sam. Come on."

Grumbling, he wriggled off the bed and stood. He was disheveled and unshaven as he stared down at her. Even in this state, he was so achingly handsome.

"Sweetheart," she whispered, sliding her hand to cup his jaw. She moved slowly, understanding he was raw and wracked with pain. Caressing his cheek with her thumb, she willed the tears in her eyes to abate. "Do you realize you're breaking my heart?"

A ragged breath exited his lungs as he shook his head. "It's what's best for you, Glarys. You'll see that one day. I'm choosing to end this so you can be with someone whole."

"Hogwash," she said, wrinkling her nose. "I have no desire to be with anyone but you. And I'll remind you that *I* get to choose whom I love, so you can stop making choices for me right now."

"Do you really want to sign up for this?" Flailing his stubbed arms, he appeared incensed. "A life with a man who can never touch you? Never hold you? I'm helpless, Glarys. A damn invalid. I'm doing you a favor, whether you realize it or not."

Furious, she stomped her foot. "First of all, you can touch me just fine."

"No, I can't—"

"Yes, you can." Standing on her toes, she kissed him, reveling in his quick intake of breath. "See? You just touched me with those magnificent lips. You'll have to use those more. I think I'll like that just fine."

Brown irises darted between hers. "I won't become a burden to you."

Rolling her eyes, she pulled the papers from her purse. "Nolan gave me these," she said, shaking them. "Did you even look at the research he did on the prosthetic limbs? They're absolutely amazing, Sam. They have the capability to do everything a functioning arm can do."

"And you'll be stuck with a man who looks like a damn cyborg."

"Like Luke Skywalker," she said, feeling herself grin. "I thought his mechanical arm was quite fancy. You'll be like the last Jedi. Like *my* Jedi. I'd be honored to be at your side while you sport something like that."

Lowering his gaze, he studied the floor, looking so forlorn that she set her purse down and slid her palms over his pecs. Closing her eyes, she shivered as the tiny hairs scratched her skin.

"Goddess, Sam," she whispered, "I feel like I haven't touched you in so long." Lifting her lids, her gaze bore into his. "I love you, you daft man. Whether you have a hundred arms or zero. Don't you understand?"

Lowering his forehead to hers, he shook his head. "Glarys, if I truly loved you, wouldn't I let you go? I feel like it's so selfish to tie you to someone who's broken."

"You're not broken. Please don't say that. You're the man who regenerated my heart. I never thought I'd ever feel love or desire again. You've given me the world, Sam. I just need you to love me enough to stay."

"I love you more than I ever thought possible," he whispered, brushing a kiss across her lips. "I'm just terrified you'll be sacrificing so much to be with me."

"Love requires sacrifice, sweetheart." Sliding her arms around his neck, she drew him close. "Will times be hard? Sure. Can we get through them together? I believe we can. The question is, do *you* believe we can?"

He was quiet for a moment. "I believe in you."

Feeling her lips curve, she drew him closer. "That's enough for now. Let's start there. We'll forge this new path together. I don't care if it's hard. I just care that you're by my side."

He studied her in silence as his shoulders slowly released their tension.

"Okay," he whispered, pushing his body into hers. "I wish I could hold you."

"I've got you," she said, squeezing her arms around his neck as their bodies molded together. "And you're doing just fine, Sam. Now, do me a favor and kiss me, will you?"

Cementing her lips to his, she threaded her fingers through his hair and succumbed to his skillful tongue. Feeling her knees buckle, she held on for dear life, so thrilled to be in his presence.

Once she'd been thoroughly kissed and blood was pounding through her veins, she drew back and bent to search her purse. Finding the box, she lifted it.

"I found this in Heden's drawer."

"I wanted to give it to you by the river. I had it all planned out. It was going to be perfect."

"Life gets in the way of perfect sometimes," she said, setting the box on his bedside table. "I'll leave it there, and you can figure out another time to give it to me. How does that sound?"

His lips curved. "It sounds pretty good." Stepping toward her, he leaned down and nuzzled her temple with his nose. "Everything inside me is reaching for you right now, honey. I wish you could feel it."

"I do," she whispered, sliding her arms around his waist. "I feel it, Sam. Now, kiss me again and tell me you love me."

Chuckling, he placed a poignant kiss on her lips. "I love you so much, Glarys. To the bottom of my soul. I hope I'm worth the struggle. I promise I'll try."

"The struggle makes the good times better—I've learned that over the centuries. We'll do this together, Sam. All the way."

Pressing his lips to hers, he drew her to him, sucking her tongue into his mouth and bathing her with his taste.

"Oh, yes," she murmured, feeling the slickness at her core. "We're going to do just fine, Sam."

Breathing a laugh, he nodded and kissed her into oblivion.

# *Chapter 12*

### *One Month Later*

Glarys watched her lover as he tested the prosthetic arms with Nolan. After some urging, Sam had agreed to try the contraptions and quickly became enthralled by them. With the human technology Nolan had employed, the circle placed on the stubs of his arms picked up nerve signals from the muscles beneath. From there, he could dictate the arms to perform several functions: grabbing, pinching, wiggling—nothing was off-limits. More exciting than the new abilities was the look on his handsome face as he realized his true capabilities.

"Okay, Sam, reach down and pick up the apple and place it next to the orange," Nolan said, gesturing to the fruit on the counter.

Sam followed the instructions, grinning the entire time. "I think I've got the hang of it, doc."

"I think you do," Nolan said, grinning. "And how about the sensations from the fingertips? Can you feel the skin of the apple?"

"Sure can. I'd like to try it on something else."

"Go for it."

Sauntering toward Glarys, he lifted the arm and brushed the prosthetic fingers over her collarbone.

"Oh, that feels nice," she said, beaming up at him.

"I can feel the softness of your skin," he murmured. "It's amazing."

"See? There's always a way, sweetheart. And you look pretty sexy with those Jedi arms."

Waggling his eyebrows, he cupped her shoulder. "We can test them out later tonight with some adult activities, if you'd like?"

"Shh..." Swatting his chest, Glarys felt her cheeks burning. "Nolan can hear you."

"Can't hear a thing," Nolan teased as he typed notes into Sam's electronic medical record on the laptop atop the counter.

"Will I be able to shoot a gun, doc?"

"Yes," Nolan said, turning and leaning back against the counter. "You'll need to practice to retrain the muscles, but you should eventually be able to aim and shoot just as effectively as before."

"Thank the goddess. I want to keep protecting my very pretty ward."

Glarys winked at him, delighted by the compliment.

"How about my knees? Can I still kneel?"

"Why would your knees be affected?" Glarys asked, feeling her eyebrows draw together.

Reaching into his pocket, he withdrew a felt box and lowered to one knee. Tears welled in Glarys's eyes as he opened it, fangs exposed as he smiled up at her.

"Just making sure because I want to do this right."

Glarys lifted a shaking hand over her lips.

"Glarys, Daughter of Davel, I never even thought I could love someone as deeply as I love you. You shattered every notion that existed about companionship and devotion. I'd be real honored if you'd agree to bond with me so I can spend eternity thanking you for everything you've given me. What do you say?"

"Yes!" she cried, clutching his face as tears streamed down her cheeks. "I love you so much, Sam."

The prosthetic fingers were deft as he slipped the ring on her finger and stood to kiss her. "Thank you, honey. You've made me so happy."

Nolan and Sadie clapped behind them, and Glarys realized she must've stepped in to observe the proposal. Embracing Sam, she smiled at the kind doctors over his shoulder. Filled with anticipation of the future they would create together, she embraced her magnificent Vampyre, overcome with joy. Not so long ago, she'd felt an aching loneliness deep inside. Now, she'd found the other half of her soul.

Sending a silent, thankful prayer to Etherya, she swayed in Sam's arms, excited to spend the centuries ahead by his side—her magnificent, soulful bonded mate.

# Epilogue

Glarys was exhausted by the time the last guest left Astaria after the reception. The bonding ceremony was lovely. She and Sam had exchanged vows under the white altar covered with flowers by the River Thayne. The reception overflowed with a multitude of food and wine, accompanied by Heden's DJ skills as he stood in the booth at the head of the room and pumped out the tunes. Now, she and Sam had retired to her room—their room now—and she sucked in a breath as she removed her heels.

"You okay?" he asked, rubbing her arm.

Nodding, she sat on the bed and began to massage her feet. "Those shoes were so pretty, but they squished the heck out of my feet. I'm happy to be rid of them."

"Here," he said, sitting beside her and pulling her feet to rest atop his thighs. "Let me do this, honey." The agile fingers of his prosthetics moved as he sent her to heaven with his ministrations.

"Oh, my," she sighed, closing her eyes and leaning back against the pillows. "That's wonderful, Sam."

He massaged her for a while before she took note of the growing desire in his hooded gaze. Feeling her body begin to hum with arousal, she crooked her finger at him.

"Why don't you move a bit higher?"

Chuckling, he grasped her hand and pulled her to stand. Leisurely, they removed their clothes, letting the anticipation intensify. When they were naked, she removed each of his prosthetics, gently setting them on the dresser before returning to his side. He slid over the sheets, resting his back against the headboard, and reached for her. He was so achingly beautiful, the stubs of his arms completely healed as he held them open. Gliding over him, she rubbed her slick center over his engorged cock, loving his desirous hiss.

"You're drenching me, sweetheart," he murmured.

"What can I say? Looking at you naked gets my body humming."

Chuckling, he squirmed below her. "Me too. Come on, honey. Ride me. I'm dying for you."

Reaching between them, she gripped his cock, rubbing the sensitive head over her opening before slowly taking him inside her quivering body. Ragged breaths filled the room as she began to move over his smooth skin. Whispering her name, he undulated his hips, pushing so deep inside her he stimulated the sensitive spot that held a thousand tiny nerve endings. Cupping his shoulder, she slid her free hand to her clit, circling her fingers over the swollen nub as desire flamed in his eyes.

"Yes, honey," he said, a muscle clenching in his jaw. "You look so pretty when you play with yourself like that. Goddess, you feel so good."

"I love you," she whispered, leaning forward to cement her lips to his.

Their bodies moved in tandem as she trailed kisses over his cheek before heading lower. Extending her tongue to lick his neck, she coated him with her saliva to shield him from the pain. Placing her fangs against his vein, she plunged them into his skin, groaning when his cock surged inside her. He uttered muted curses against her skin as he repeated her ministrations with his tongue upon her neck. She felt the scrape of his fangs against her wet skin a second before he pierced her, moaning in pleasure as her blood invaded his mouth.

They were joined in every possible way, his shaft claiming her as they imbibed each other's essence. Threading her fingers through his thick hair, she rode him in a blissful dream that was somehow now reality. The movement of their hips increased until she felt her orgasm on the horizon. Purring against his neck, she gave in to the pleasure, feeling her body snap as he hammered into her. Lost to pleasure, she held on for dear life as jets of his release coated her core. Breaking contact with his neck, she buried her face against his skin and rode the magnificent wave.

Slowly, they came back to Earth, licking each other's wounds to aid the self-healing properties. Slick and sweaty, they held each other for what seemed like hours until she felt his release slip between them.

"Be right back," she murmured, gently pecking his cheek. Sliding off his lap, she trailed to the bathroom, returning with a wet cloth to clean them both.

Tossing the cloth in the hamper a moment later, she joined him in bed, pulling the covers over their cooling bodies as she rested her cheek on his chest. Gently, Sam caressed her upper back with the stub of his right arm, which extended to where his elbow once began. Closing her eyes, Glarys reveled in the tender strokes, so proud he'd conquered his fears and doubts. As sleep began to sink its claws into her consciousness, she mumbled against his chest.

"I'm so honored to be your bonded mate, Sam."

He sighed beneath her, the action filled with reverence. "Glarys, you have no idea how happy you've made me. I was so sure it was over for me, but you saved me from myself. I wish I could repay you. Since I can't, I'll just love you in every way I know how and with every cell in my body. I swear, I'm going to do everything in my power to put you first."

"You already do," she said, overcome with emotion at his tender words. "You're perfect, sweetheart. One day, you'll realize that. For now, I'll just hold the sentiment deep in my heart."

Firm lips placed worshipful kisses on her forehead as her eyes drifted shut. Enveloped in her bonded's loving embrace, Glarys yielded to the darkness, firm in the knowledge Sam would be there when she eventually returned to the light.

## Before You Go

Well, dear readers, I hope you enjoyed Glarys and Sam's love story! If you enjoyed meeting Lila and Latimus in this book, their story is told in Book 2 of the series, **The Elusive Sun**. And you can continue on to read Book 6, **The Cryptic Prophecy**, now! Thanks so much for spending some time in Etherya's Earth with me!

# *Acknowledgments*

Thanks to Bryony for the fantastic editing and proofreading, and to Anthony for the wonderful cover.

And thanks to each and every one of you for reading my books.

# ALSO BY REBECCA HEFNER

### Prevent the Past Series
Book 1: A Paradox of Fates
Book 2: A Destiny Reborn
Book 3: A Timeline Restored

### The Etherya's Earth Series
Prequel: The Dawn of Peace
Book 1: The End of Hatred
Book 2: The Elusive Sun
Book 3: The Darkness Within
Book 4: The Reluctant Savior
Book 4.5: Immortal Beginnings
Book 5: The Impassioned Choice
Book 5.5: Two Souls United
Book 6: The Cryptic Prophecy
Book 6.5: Garridan's Mate
Book 7: Coming soon!

# About the Author

USA Today bestselling author Rebecca Hefner grew up in Western NC and now calls the Hudson River of NYC home. In her youth, she would sneak into her mother's bedroom and read the romance novels stashed on the bookshelf, cementing her love of HEAs. A huge Buffy and Star Wars fan, she loves an epic fantasy and a surprise twist (Luke, he IS your father).

Before becoming an author, Rebecca had a successful twelve-year medical device sales career. After launching her own indie publishing company, she is now a full-time author who loves writing strong, complex characters who find their

HEAs. Rebecca can usually be found making dorky and/or embarrassing posts on TikTok and Instagram. Please join her so you can laugh along with her!

Made in the USA
Coppell, TX
14 February 2022

73584892R00088